The Adventures of Horatio Woosencraft and Other Stories

Seán Thomas Kane

The Adventures of Horatio Woosencraft
and Other Stories

First Edition.

Published by the Author, 2017.

"Abducted and Abandoned" first published
by the author through
Kindle Direct Publishing, 2014.

sthosdkane.com

Other books by the author

Abducted and Abandoned
Travels in Time Across Europe

TABLE OF CONTENTS

The Adventures of

Horatio Woosencraft

Prologue

Just how I came to meet
Mr. Horatio Woosencraft

In the city of Kansas City, in County Jackson there lived a gentleman by the name of Horatio Woosencraft. Now Mr. Woosencraft lived on Warwick Boulevard. I too lived there for a time, as his assistant when he was at the prime of his practise, just after the War in Iraq had ended. Now Woosencraft as I shall furthermore call him was not your usual sort of gentleman, he was known for his antique tastes, he enjoyed baroque music, wore a top hat and overcoat when out and a tailcoat when in. It was as though he were from sometime in the recent past, yet not the present. Now he had never had a real profession, occasionally dabbling in many areas when I knew him he dabbled in law, music, theatre, botany, architecture, painting, sculpture, golf and fencing, all of which he was exemplary at, much more so than myself. Despite his immense talents his real passion was crime.

I first met him at boarding school. It was my first day there and I came upon this talented young gentleman playing the violin with a splendid manner. I approached him after he finished Strauss's *Kaiser-Walzer*, "Pardon me sir," I said in the most polite manner possible, "that was the grandest way of playing that piece I've yet heard."

He looked at me, no reaction on his face, his features as silent as a grave. The poor lad was quite pale; he had dark brown hair that was parted at one point on the left side of his head. He wore his school uniform in full, the coat was on, the shoes were shined, yet he had that cold lonely feeling about him, and he stared at me with those dark deep black eyes of his, eyes that seemed to search my face and my appearance as though reading my complexion. "I see 'tis your first time away from home," he said, turning his eyes to look deep into my own, "well is it not sir?"

"That it is sir," I replied confused as any young boy of fourteen would be,

"Yet how do you know sir?"

"Your upper lip quivers," he replied, he had an accent that sounded vaguely Welsh, "and your eyes seem to dart about the place like those men who come over here alone, I remember them from the dock in New York. Tell me," said he with great kindness, "what's your name?"

"Theodore Carroll's my name sir, I'm from Weston, Missouri," I replied, with speed."

"Uh hmn, and your father I take it is the Attorney General for the State of Missouri?" He replied.

I was stunned, how could such a person know, "Why... y-yes he is... but h-how sir do you know?" I stammered.

"Tell me sir, have you no knowledge of hereditarily resemblance's?!" exclaimed the amazed young gentleman before me, "It's obvious is it not, you are the striking image of your dear father, Honourable Justice Ignatius Carroll. I thought you might just be his son from when you first entered the room, yet when you stated your name I knew you were his son. By the way, Horatio Woosencraft, Second Year." He held out his hand, and I took it, as we shook hands I wondered, just where this man of such knowledge originated, yet did not ask anymore of him for fear of insulting the gentleman.

He would graduate a year ahead of me yet I still admired him, becoming his main friend, actually his only friend throughout all his years at Dafydd Sant. Now during those years he showed his talents in the area of crime. We went on many an adventure on the school grounds, solving crimes committed by students and teachers alike. It was the first of these mysteries that he solved during my time at Dafydd that was quite memorable.

The Adventure of the Headmaster's Wallet

It was during the first semester of that year, 2007, when a most peculiar occurrence came to pass. The entire school had gone to Kansas City for a school trip to see our own Dafydd Sant Soccer team take on the Saint Jerome High School team. Now as the match was going on, the Headmaster of our school happened to be robbed of a great sum of money. I was watching the match from our crowd, looking at the pitch as was everyone else, not caring for anything else at that time, when I heard that familiar Welsh accent, "Mr. Carroll, would you care to join me in an… adventure of sorts?"

I turned then, Woosencraft stood there in his uniform, looking straight at me with the same expressionless face. I thought what if I'm caught away from our crowd? But adventure, one could use some adventure, but if I get in trouble, what'll father say? "Show me t-the way Woosencraft," I said firmly. He led me away from our cheering section up to the walkway behind the teacher's section. Upon our arrival he pulled me back behind a column, which he too used as cover. I surveyed his face then, the lad was again expressionless, amazing that no expression could come out of that cold hard face.

"Do you see the Headmaster there?" he said, pointing at the man.

"Yes, what of him?"

"Describe what you see to me Mr. Carroll," he commanded. Now at the time I wondered whether or not he was a teacher in disguise or something of that sort, yet I did as was commanded, "Well he's wearing that usual bowler hat with the overcoat, good thing too," said I with a shiver for 'twas very cold that evening. "He appears to be watching the game Woosencraft," I said more irritated now, "why come up here for, why watch him?"

"Do you see his coat pocket on the left?"

"Yes Woosencraft, what about it?"

"Do you see the black leather object sticking out of it?"

"Yes, but what's the," I stopped and looked at Woosencraft, "tell me has his wallet been stolen or something?"

"Excellent deduction Mr. Carroll, as a matter a fact it has, I saw the gentleman walking away with his real wallet, the one in there is a fake."

"So who stole it, did you know the man?"

"Yes I did as a matter of fact," he said then with a sharp breath was silent, for a number of teachers were walking by at that moment. Woosencraft then stepped out from our place of hiding and crept over towards the Headmaster. I moved suddenly, and Woosencraft turned, looking at me in the eye he put a finger to his lips, signaling me to be a silent observer of him at work. He crept up behind the Headmaster and slipped the wallet from the pocket, then turned and walked back in a regular pace. Returning to our sanctuary he showed me the wallet, upon opening it we found that it had a set of initials sewn in gold thread into it, DFG. "You see Carroll, our thief has mad a grave mistake by having a wallet engraved with his initials put into the pocket."

Soon the Headmaster realised his wallet had been stolen, yet by then we were far from the scene. I followed Woosencraft as he made his way back towards where the coach was to take us back to

Dafydd Sant. Whilst on the coach ride back to school I noticed the strangest thing yet about this gentleman, the fact that he sat completely still the entire journey, not once speaking to another soul onboard. He's always been a lonely man, yet especially during his school years, when he would not speak for days. As we got back off the coach he passed a small piece of paper into my hand, then walked on into the building. I read the fine cursive handwriting of that lonely soul, the sorrowful beauty of the letters curving on the paper, how the ink had left a lasting impression on the paper, just as the writer had left a lasting impression on me. "Meet me in the Llywelyn Fawr[1] common room tonight at exactly 11.00."

I did as was requested, coming to the Llywelyn Fawr Common Room at that time. Now I should explain Dafydd Sant is divided into houses named for certain Welsh figures, there's Llywelyn Fawr, my own house named for Llywelyn the Great, there's Owain Gwynedd, named for the former's grandfather, there's Rhodri Mawr, named for Rhodri the Great, and David Lloyd George, named for the British Prime Minister commonly known as the "Welsh Wizard". Woosencraft was also in Llywelyn Fawr, yet was distanced from the rest of the house through out his years at Dafydd Sant. Upon entering the common room I at first saw no one there, the fire still crackled in the hearth, yet not a soul was to be found within my vision. Then I heard the voice, "I see you've come… Mr. Carroll. I thought you wouldn't come."

---

[1] Llywelyn the Great, a Welsh king of the Twelfth and Thirteenth Centuries Anno Domini

I walked towards the wingback from whence the voice came, to find the young gentleman sitting there, staring at the flames, the crackle of the fire as it incinerates the wood, the occasional collapse of some of the wood, which uproots sparks like angry bees when a bees' nest is disturbed. There before sat the lonely gentleman Woosencraft, its light breaking through the darkness like a ship beaks through the North Atlantic ice. I now know him well enough to state truthfully that he was most like the room in which we met that night. He was all a cold sorrowful soul, except for that light that shone through the darkness, that light which was crime, solving mysteries. He sat there, still as one of Her Majesty's guards, not even turning to look at me as I came to sit beside him in the darkened chamber.

With a sudden movement he rose from the chair, and strode towards the door leading into the corridor beyond. I sat and watched him, he walked with a sense of duty, a sense that I hadn't seen in anyone ever before. As he reached the door he turned, saw I was still in my chair, and made the first facial expression I would ever see him make, as his left eyebrow rose, he said, "Well Mr. Carroll, are you not coming?"

I arose quickly, realising just what he was saying, following him out of the common room into the corridor beyond. We strode briskly through the school until we reached the school library. It was here that Woosencraft finally stopped; his face seemed to glow in the darkness of the library. Walking amongst the shelves I felt a shiver of fear run down my spine, the place was of a state that would frighten even the most courageous of men after hours. It reminded me of the tales my grandfather used to tell, years ago when I was just a lad of five years. Now he had come over from England in the year 1951, with no more than twenty dollars in his pocket. He'd tell the tales of how it was said that the great old buildings of the world were home to both the living and the dead, and how if you weren't careful they would spring out at you from the darkness. I thought on Robert Burns' famed poem *Tam O'Shanter*, of how in the darkness Tam came upon a circle of witches dancing to the devil's own pipes.

As we walked further into the library we came to hear the most peculiar of sounds, of a gentleman slowly scraping away at some isolated part of the wall. Woosencraft motioned for me to halt, and he drew quickly a flashlight from his coat pocket. He crept up behind the man before us saying to the shock of the man, "Can I help you find something sir?"

The man jumped, and spun around only to have the flashlight shining in his eyes. He squinted, attempting to get a glimpse of Woosencraft yet to no avail. Woosencraft, using the calmest of tones as though he were in an armchair relaxing and having small talk with other persons, said, "Tell me about that wallet you stole."

The man looked up at Woosencraft; his face showed some shock upon it.

"I, I d-don't" he stammered, "I d-don't know what you're talking about sir!" he exclaimed, trying to run off, yet was pinned to the floor by Woosencraft who looked at me saying, "Look into that hole there in the wall."

I did as was told and to my astonishment found a small leather object, in the process of being hidden within the wall. It was a fine article, one which appeared to have been owned at some point by a man of great distinction. I shook with amazement, "T-the wallet, look Woosencraft, the Headmaster's wallet!"

"And just where did you get that Mr. Carroll?" asked a voice which made my hairs raise.

"Mr. Gruffydd," said Woosencraft calmly, "it is an honour to be in your presence sir."

"Enough of those niceties Mr. Woosencraft!" shouted Gruffydd, "Come along you three, to the Headmaster's quarters."

"But sir," said the robber, "please I had no part in this sir."

"All three of you," repeated Gruffydd, "and that includes you too Mr. Thomas."

We walked along the corridors at a swift pace, behind Gruffydd by some five feet. The man was the last person on Earth, save the Headmaster himself and my Father who I'd want to meet with at that time of night. He was the head of the Welsh language department at Dafydd Sant, whose great sense of nationalism made him quite a hothead both outside the classroom and within its confines. He walked at a quick march pace, just like a soldier. I had heard rumors of his service in the Falklands but those hadn't been confirmed.

I whispered to Woosencraft, who was still calm despite the grave case we were in. "How did you know it was in the Library?" asked I.

"I overheard Thomas at dinner tonight, he said he had to go to the Library later to drop some stuff off," he replied.

"Alright, but how did you know that Hugh Thomas had the wallet in the first place?"

"Because he left his ID in the wallet," he calmly replied. "I found it in there on the coach on the way back to school."

"So how did you know he was to drop the wallet off at the library, he could have been dropping off some books or something of that sort."

"You know as well as I do that the Library is not open after dinner," he replied, "So I took a guess to say that he was in the mindset to drop off something else, something stolen. It's the oldest part of the building, the walls are weaker there, he would have been able to cut a hole in a wall in the Library and store the wallet in the hole."

"Quiet back there!" shouted Gruffydd, the symbol of hypocrisy. We reached the Headmaster's quarters, entering to find the Headmaster in his robe, looking very stern.
"Now what's brought you to awaken me from my sleep Mr. Gruffydd?" he asked.

"I've found your wallet on these boys Owen," Gruffydd stated.

"My wallet eh?" asked the Headmaster with surprise, "and these boys have it?"

"Yes sir," I said, handing it to him in submission.

"Ah Mr. Carroll, I'd have thought better of you. I'll of course be writing to your father about this," he said, then turning to Thomas next, "Mr. Thomas the same for you," he then turned towards Woosencraft and with a sorrowful look on his face, "As for you Mr. Woosencraft, I'd have thought better of you, however seeing as you have no family I shall have to write to Sir Banastre, however I must also ask you just how you came to possess this wallet."

I was stunned, Woosencraft an orphan? No wonder the coldness of his being; he was filled with sorrow and grief. "Sir," he said as calm as ever, "I was standing behind the teacher's box at the soccer match at Saint Jerome, and I saw someone walk by you and slip your wallet out of your pocket and replace it with a different wallet. Now I stood there watching to see if he'd come back at all, figuring that he would not. I soon decided to go and get my friend," he looked at me, I realised I was his only friend ever, "Carroll. We went back to where I'd been standing and I chose to act. I snuck up behind you and took the wallet left by the robber from you pocket, we then left to go to the coach because the game was nearly over.

"On the coach I opened the wallet, to look for any sign of the robber confined within it. I have it here with me," he said withdrawing it from his pocket. "What I beheld was the ID of the robber, a foolish thing for any person wishing to steal anything to do, leaving their ID behind."

"So who's ID was it Mr. Woosencraft?" asked the Headmaster.

"Oh do you actually believe the boy! Come now Owen is that not taking it a bit too far?" snorted Gruffydd.

"There may be facts within this tale that Mr. Woosencraft is telling," the Headmaster replied, "Please Mr. Woosencraft, continue."

"Thank you sir. Now tonight at dinner I overheard Thomas saying that he had to go down to the Library later tonight, yet I knew just as well as he did that the Library is not open after dinner. I chose to take Carroll down there to intercept Thomas in the Library and see what he was up to. Upon entering the Library we heard some scratching noises coming from one of the corners, Carroll and I walked quietly towards the noise, finding a man bent over trying to scrape away at wallpaper and wall itself. I shined this flashlight," he held up his flashlight to show to the Headmaster and Gruffydd, "at his head saying 'May I help you with something sir?' He spun around and I discovered the man to be none other than Hugh Thomas. Now Carroll here bent down to look in the hole carved by Thomas. In it he found none other than the wallet owned by your honour."

"I didn't do it," said Thomas quickly, "I didn't steal the wallet, I was just supposed to hide it."

"Then who stole the wallet Mr. Thomas?" asked the Headmaster.

"I-I cannot say sir," he replied.

"Mr. Thomas, you must tell us, it'll only bring about good results," replied the Headmaster.

"Sir, I cannot tell you who, they'll hurt me if I did."

"Oh very well," said the Headmaster, "however I think you should be punished for the damage to school property Mr. Thomas, and for not giving my wallet back to me as you should have done. Detention Mr. Thomas, tomorrow evening with Mr. Gruffydd."

Thomas looked as though he were about to die of fear, I wished I could say something on his behalf, however the Headmaster dismissed Woosencraft and I back to our common room.

When we got back we remained in front of the fire for some time, I looked into those sorrowful eyes, feeling pity for my friend. "Woosencraft," I said, "Why did you not tell me about your family?"

He looked at me, teary eyed, "B-because Carroll, because I don't like to talk about it. I hate my past, I hate where I came from, and I hate criminals."

"What happened?" I asked with pity for the sorrowful in my voice.

"When I was but six years of age," he began, the tears now rolling down his cheeks, those which the floodgates of his military like lack of emotion had held back for these many years, "my father was forced out of his work in a mine, he went on strike. My mother worried every day about him, and one day her worries were at last confirmed. A man called on our home one day, he was the mine owner. My father was the leader of the strikers. Now the mine owner went into the drawing room to talk to my father about ending the strike. The conversation became violent, and then I heard the mine owner's voice shouting,

"You Welsh dog! You are my miner! Mine!" He beat my father, who fought back. As I stood in the doorway I watched, as the mine owner drew a handgun from his suit and pointed it straight at my dear father.

"I loved my father Carroll," he said through his sobs, "I l-l-loved him-m. And that criminal t-took h-him from m-me, h-his s-son. My mother soon went down the mines in my father's place; she died in a cave in last year. I was the only one left, and I came here to Dafydd Sant, where I was given shelter, and a new home and life."

I sat there in the silence starring at my friend, my sorrowful friend. He seemed to have gone through so much that I wondered if he was really alive any longer. "Theodore," he said, now this was the first time I heard him use my first name, "you are my family now, my brother, and only friend."

I was shocked at what I'd heard that night from Woosencraft. Now since that fateful night we have become close friends and confidants, but when I remember that night, tears still come to my eyes. A great and immense sorrow filled my friend, a sorrow created by what he sought to end, crime. For the rest of his life, he would go on to fight crime in full. It was that first crime which we were to encounter together that set the course for our friendship. We continued our search for the thief of the wallet. Every evening we'd meet in the common room and Woosencraft would ask me, "So Carroll, any luck today in finding Thomas' friends?"

For many days the response was the negative, I'd spent all my free time following Thomas about the building. Documenting each and every one of his friends and those to whom he regularly spoke. After the third week of this Thomas began to cease to appear in the corridors of Dafydd Sant, and rumors began to spread that he was confining himself to the David Lloyd George common room. One such evening when Woosencraft and I sat before the fire together, after all others had retired for the night, I told my friend of the situation, "Woosencraft," I said, "my job is only getting harder by the day. Thomas hasn't been seen outside of the David Lloyd George common room for sometime, it's impossible for me to watch his movements any longer."

"Ah my dear Carroll," he said in a matter-of-fact fashion, "you may be at a dead end however what you've been doing has only helped our investigation."

"But how Woosencraft?" I asked, as my eyebrows rose.

"I wanted you to watch him and his confidants for two reasons. First to record who he meets with most commonly and most unusually. You have succeeded in a certain fashion in that charge. Secondly I wished for you to do that so you could get him out of the ferret's hole. Now that he's retreated into the David Lloyd George common room we know where whoever stole the wallet will go to speak to him." As he spoke I heard the corridor door opening behind us, I stood quickly and spun around to face the intruder, but Woosencraft calmly said, "Worry not my friend, this is our eyes and ears in the David Lloyd George common room, you know Mr. Ioan Aelsby, do you not?"

He was a second year, about six feet tall with a slim body and fair composure in the face. We shook hands as I said, "A pleasure to meet you sir."

"And the same to you Mr. Carroll," he replied, his voice was like a croak coming from a frog or a toad, as though he had some sort of a cold or fever.

"Woosencraft," he said turning to my friend, "I've been watching the common room as you requested, and have observed some meetings between Mr. Hugh Thomas and other persons, however none of these meetings are secretive, all but one. As I sat in the common room working on my essay on *The Four Branches of the Mabinogi*, I saw out of the corner of my eye Thomas meeting with another student, they went into a corner and spoke in whispers. After a while the other student went to leave and I called him over to my table saying, 'Pardon me sir but do you recall what the name of the King of Ireland was in *Branwen, Daughter of Llŷr?*' he replied saying, 'His name was Matholwch.' I asked for the gentleman's name so I could put it into my bibliography, and would you believe it, he gave it to me!"

"And?!" exclaimed I, "Who was it?!"

Woosencraft however was not looking at the two of us, he stared in the direction of the door, where another person had just entered. "It was good of you to give Aelsby here your name sir," he said to the person who'd just entered the chamber.

Mr. Gruffydd stepped forward, his face full of a rage, "And I should've thought better of it before I gave it away," he said scathingly. "I'll have the three of you out of Dafydd Sant so quickly you wouldn't even realise you'd left. He seemed ready to charge us like a bull, the fury in those red eyes, so much hatred amassed up because of what we could do to him if the Headmaster found out. He walked to the fire and grabbed a poker from next to it, and raised it towards us, ready to strike Woosencraft. He swung it down upon my good friend, yet I moved so quickly into the line of fire as to divert the blow and take it for myself. I crumpled to the floor and remembered no more.

~

When my friend Carroll was hit I reacted as any friend would. I quickly shouted to Aelsby saying, "Ioan, get the Headmaster quickly now."

"But what are you going to do Woosencraft?" he asked me, shocked at what he had just seen. "Just go, get the headmaster."

He quickly ran out the door, before Gruffydd could stop him. It was just him and I in the chamber together, he punched me in the gut, and I fell to the ground next to my friend, who lay unconscious. "Your father was just the same

Woosencraft," he sneered, "Always getting into other people's business. He died just as you are about to, a fool, who tried to ruin the fortunes of others."

"You knew my father?!"

"Oh yes I knew him, I set up his death," jeered the teacher.

I cursed as I've never done before at him, attempting to get up and beat him over the head into submission. My fury at the man who had arranged the death of my father was greater than all the armies of the nations, greater than the mines within which my dear father had once worked, where my dear mother had died. My forcefulness to get my revenge at him was great, and I lunged forward trying to knock him to the ground avenge my father's death.

"When he started the strike I lost my job, I was supposed to keep him in line, and the fired me. I was evicted from my home because I couldn't pay taxes, and knew I needed to enact my revenge on the man who had ruined my life. I told the owner of the mine that he should 'deal' with your dear father personally, that he should kill the man. The man was more than happy to do just that, and he succeeded. I danced with joy upon hearing the news. I had vanquished my worst rival, and had won over him."

I screamed at him, "You killed him! You killed my father, you killed my innocence that day!"

As I screamed at Gruffydd the door opened again and the Headmaster entered with Aelsby, shock and rage upon his face at what he saw before him. Behind him came two policemen, their handguns drawn and aimed at Gruffydd.

"Drop the poker," firmly said the Headmaster. "Drop it or these men shall fire."

Now a sensible man would drop the arm, a stubborn man would remain with it yet lose their life, yet a coward and hypocrite would drop it and beg for mercy, just as Gruffydd did that night. He was handcuffed and as they were about to take him from the chamber I asked him, "What was the owner's name?"

He turned to look at me, the fire still in his eyes, yet he seemed very tired all the same, "Jones," he said, "He is named Jones." Then he was led out of the chamber. I then attended to my friend, he was still unconscious, and we decided to take him to a nearby hospital.

~

I awoke with the feeling that I'd fallen from the top of Mount Snowdon onto my forehead. My eyesight was quite blurry when I awoke, however my mind was sharp. I quickly sat up in my bed, remarking as soon as I'd done it that it had been a poor course of action, for my head now felt as though it'd been hit by a gong or frying pan. "What happened, where's Gruffydd?" I looked to my right to see my friend sitting in a chair looking at me, "W-woosencraft, what happened last night? Where's Gruffydd, we need to stop him before he gets away!"

"Worry not my friend," Woosencraft soothingly replied, "Gruffydd hit you upside the head when you jumped in front of me; saving my own head from a concussion. Gruffydd was apprehended by the Headmaster and two policemen. Everything is all right, worry not my friend."

"And where is Gruffydd now?" I asked.

"He is in court, charged with the attempted murders of Horatio Woosencraft and Theodore Carroll, also being charged with child abuse, theft, and harassment. I figure he'll be imprisoned for life after this one. We are to be awarded for our service to the school, in keeping a felon out of the school. Aelsby is to thank for some of that, however I did have a strong feeling that Gruffydd was behind it all in the first place."

"But how is that and if so why did we have to go through Thomas to get to him?"

"Because he knew I was onto him, but he could not do anything outright to me, except for get me into detention, and expulsion. Did you notice the look on his face when we gave the Headmaster back his wallet?"

"No, what'd he look like?"

"His face when all white, I knew then that he'd stolen the wallet, whilst you were watching Thomas on his rounds, I was notifying the Headmaster on Gruffydd's movements. I knew he was going to the David Lloyd George common room even before Aelsby did. Aelsby was just a cover up for my actions. Our plan was to lure Gruffydd into the common room that night when we met, using Aelsby as bait. It worked and within the hour we had our culprit caught."

I would recover that night and was back at Dafydd Sant the next day, though bandaged on the head, I was recognised along with Woosencraft and Aelsby by the Headmaster. Woosencraft would not tell me of what he and Gruffydd discussed whilst I was unconscious for many years, until it would become prevalent to our work. It was in this way that we solved our first case together, the Case of the Headmaster's Wallet.

What happened after Dafydd Sant

and how Woosencraft and I were to meet again.

Many years passed. Woosencraft graduated in 2010 and went on to Oxford where I hear he did quite well, graduating after three years with doctorates in History, Music, Forensic Science, Theology, and Celtic Languages. I would go on to Oxford as well, yet my good friend always eluded me during my years there. It was not until some three years after my own graduation in 2015 from Oxford with a doctorate in History and a Masters in Music that I would meet him again.

I was living in an old house on Charlotte in Kansas City at the time. I was the head of the performing arts department at Saint Ignatius and doing quite well for myself. It was during our performance of a play known as *Fort William* that I happened to see him in the audience. He had the same basic features, except for the fact that he was older than the 15 year old who played the *Kaiser-Walzer* so well on my first day at Dafydd Sant.

Now during the intermission I went down to meet him in the foyer. There stood my good friend, Horatio Woosencraft, a genius in all forms of the term. He seemed as sorrowful as ever, yet I still was drawn to his side. As I came forth from behind him he said, "A delightful production as of yet Mr. Carroll, I am glad to see you've been faring well."

I took no offense to what he said, saying, "Woosencraft. It's so good to see you after all these years. How fares thee?"

"A slight toll on my line of work I'm afraid. I've been out of a job for the past six months."

"Out of a job?! Why Woosencraft surely not!" I exclaimed, "What with all your qualifications and such, you could be a barrister or a judge."

"Always thinking on the law still are you Carroll, after all these years your father's shadow still hangs over you like a great black cloud, covering the light from your being?"

"I'm just used to it. My father, may he rest in peace, had a great impression on me."

"Yes I understand, same as my own father, I follow his three rules: First, never back down, always move forward. Second, always let all the clues help lead you to success. Third, never discount anything, all could be of importance."

At that time a stagehand came to tell me that the show was about to begin again, and Woosencraft and I parted ways again. He convinced me to sell my house on Charlotte and move in with him, partly to help him pay the rent, and partly because I wanted to help him get his detective genius useful in creating a job for him. He lived in an old house on Warwick, its stone structure was a century old by the time I'd moved in. The place was grand in how my friend had decorated it. He had resided there alone since 2013 when he'd first came back to America from Oxford. I would live with him there for many years, and still live there now, even though he is long since gone.

The Adventure of the House of Celestians

It was in my second month in residence at No. 43 Warwick Boulevard that the most interesting of persons came to call upon Woosencraft and I. Now Woosencraft had needed help paying the taxes and heating bills for his Warwick Boulevard Residence, and it was in such circumstances that I moved into a set of rooms at No. 43.

Woosencraft remained his old self, he hadn't changed much in the past ten years, since that fateful day when the "Kaiser-Walzer" sung in the strings of his violin. He had a small trade at that time, working on pick-pocketing offences and felonies involving the rare beheaded tree. Yet his profession only kicked off when the most peculiar of women came to call, a woman of great height, yet narrow frame. She wore a shawl over her shoulders and a wide brimmed hat, old rose and all resting in its nest atop her crown. Her face was narrow, thin, the bones of her cheeks could be seen, those cheeks that shone red. Upon calling at No. 43 she knew not what to expect, and naturally showed some anguish at the proposition of speaking to two gentlemen, foreign as of that date to her, one of which was renowned for his talents in the realm of observation.

Now when she entered the drawing room, where we always met our guests, she seemed to walk with a bounce in her step, yet through all the amiable characteristics of her stride, could be seen the fear of something unknown to man's intellect.

"Mr. Woosencraft," said she, curtseying as she did, "I have come to speak to you of a most terrible situation."

She looked at me with some disgust.

"Oh yes, my dear lady, if I may introduce my associate Professor Theodore Carroll, whatever you say to me you may also say in front of him, he has my full confidence."

"My dear lady," replied the man, ever more enclosed in his thoughts "you work, I believe, in an old home do you not? Might not this be the Browne House on 67th Terrace? And your place of business is troubled is it, by someone, or something, disturbing the peace of the long vacant residence?" she appeared startled at his calculations, "Pray, do tell of your experiences."

"Well sir?" said she with such a squeak that I looked to see if a mouse were skirting along the wall directly behind her, "How could you know so much? Is it you that torments my business?!

"Fear not my dear," Woosencraft replied, "Ms Folan, I believe that is you is it not? For I am not the torment of your recent weeks and months. The mud on your shoes suggests some involvement in the outdoors, and the way in which you are wearing your hair looks somewhat, shall we say, unnatural to your common physical appearance. I figured you were the director of the house, the manager of its operations by the way in which your face went cold when I said 'someone, or something'. Now pray, please tell us your account of the recent unnatural events at the Browne House."

She took a seat in a nearby chair, her demeanour was of one who would want nothing more than to spout out some knowledge that had been burning away at her soul for weeks on end.

"Good sirs, I am as you have guessed, Bernadette Folan, the Director of the Browne House and Museum. My trade takes me to great extremes, dealing with both the public, and artefacts of great historical significance. Recently however I have had another thing, or set of things, with which I have been forced to deal with, now these are quite unnatural. I was standing in the foyer of the house when I heard a noise on the stairs, I looked up, investigating the noise, asking, 'Who's there?'

"No voice answered, but when I went up to investigate I found a pair of footprints on the landing, from where the sound had come. I stared in horror at the footprints, looking as they led up the stairs, onto the second floor. In my fear I followed, they led to the porch just above the house's front door. I watched as the footsteps made their way, onto the top of the railing, and then stopped. I then heard a soft sound, unheard by my own ears ever before, the sound of a soft and sweet song, which came from where the footprints had ceased to advance upon the railing. It was then that I heard something softly hit the doorstep below. I looked down, fearing what my eyes may lay upon, and saw no more than a pair of hand-prints, not in the muddy like the footprints that had led me to this place, but red, as though someone had made their hands bleed upon impact.

"I had only been at the house for three months, I had previously worked at the Farrow Manor in Oxfordshire. Yet no former director nor former staff or volunteer would speak of the occurrence or it's repetition. However much I feared seeing the celestial footprints again, I at the same time sought them out, looking at the landing every time I passed, yet I never again saw a thing. It was on the eleventh month of my employment that I saw yet another thing, I sat in my office, working on a press release about an event we were holding, when I spied out of the corner of my eye, a woman in the next room over, I looked closer at the place yet saw nothing. It was then that without warning I felt a pair of soothing hands on my shoulders. They rubbed my shoulders, oh how soft felt they upon my shoulders. Yet soon they got closer to my neck, closer by the moment, until they were upon my neck, grabbing at me, suffocating me, I wrenched the pair of hands off, and turned to see the woman behind me, a look of red fury in her eyes.

"Mr. Woosencraft, I know not what to do, please help me, I'm afraid to return to work, even the Farrow House was haunted, yet it was not like this."

"And do you actually think, Ms Folan, that a ghost is haunting the Browne House?"

"Sir, I know not what to think, I only know that something wrong is going on in the house."

"Madam, I will be of assistance to you," replied Woosencraft, "however I must warn you that if we do find anything within the confines of the home of the now deceased Horace Browne, I will find it a necessity to alert the authorities, thus making it a possibility for your own incarceration in the Fortescue Mental Hospital."

"Sir!"shouted the director of the foul house, "I am not a madman, despite what my tale may tell! And if one were to call me as such," she made to leave, "I shall take my business elsewhere."

"Alas my dear Carroll," said Woosencraft, "that Ms Folan could not stay for long enough to see the ghost of No. 43!"

Folan turned on her heel, fear embedded in her eyes, "T-there's a-a ghghost here! You have se-een it?!"

"But of course my dear lady, I was only making sure that you were not trying to play a hoax on me, or worse,"his face shown in full seriousness, "you had been sent as a spy by Dr William Newman of the Fortescue Mental Hospital, he has been sending some rather nasty notes of late," he motioned towards a side table covered with at least three dozen letters and envelopes.

"Miss Folan,"I began.

"It's Madam Folan," she intervened.

"Oh are you married?"I asked with an air of curiosity.

"I was, my husband died when he was on a hunting trip in Scotland, years ago," she replied, the sorrow evident in her voice.

"Oh my dear," I replied, "I am so sorry to hear, of your husband's death."

"There is no need," she replied stiffly, "Now I'd best be back to work, good day gentlemen."

"And to you, we shall be around at the house at half-past four this afternoon," replied Woosencraft, "Now madam, good day to you."

She rose and walked out of the chamber, heading down the short flight of stairs and out the door, only pausing to look at a cut mark in the wallpaper on the landing, written in script, reading: Liberæ Cambriæ.

Now Woosencraft was well known through out the scholarly community for his sense of national pride. He loved the land of his fathers. He would sometimes tell stories of his great-grandfather's role in the mine strikes of 1910, and of how his grandfather had been instrumental in founding the Welsh Nationalist Party, Plaid Cymru. Whether my friend had been born in Wales too was unknown to me at the time of the Browne House happening, and I had always thought he had been born in one of the colonies, Canada or Newfoundland, or perhaps out in the Atlantic, the stormy seas seemed to be much akin to his personality.

We sat in silence for some time, until I could not resist the question any longer, "Woosencraft, where exactly did you get your mental abilities from exactly?"

"Well Professor," he replied in his matter of fact manner, "I would say that my abilities came from my mother's side, the Pfastuch's they were, from Anglesey, my dear mother, Mary Pfastuch Woosencraft, was a keen woman, she could spot any sign of trouble a year prior to it's commencement. Her famed saying was, 'I seek no more than what is best for my kin.'"

"And what Woosencraft, do you seek?" I asked, a grin on my face.

"I crave mental recognition, the praise of the scholars of this world, the love of those who read the daily papers. I have come forth from obscurity to fame and prowess over all others in what they refer to as 'their profession', when in fact I alone created it, I alone devised it, I alone practise it. And what if one were to take this profession from me, what if one were to take my life from me? There is no more, no more I say, for me in this life, I would die with my trade, and pray for better in the next life."

"Woosencraft!" I exclaimed, "What a thing to say! I'm assured you could live without your trade, what with your talents as a violinist, you could outdo Johann Strauss II by ten-fold."

"That may be Professor," he said, "but have you thought about what life would be like if the one thing you loved, the one thing worth living for, was taken from you? You would rather remove the threat of hating your life," then seeing the look of pure anguish written upon my face he said soothingly, "Yet worry not my dear friend, for I am certain it shan't come to such an end for my own life, pray at least for the moment whilst we have the Browne House to search, which we must be on our way. Come Professor, a cab to the Browne House."

I obtained our cab, and we were quickly spirited away from Warwick Boulevard, and taken a few blocks south to the locale of the Horace Browne House. The place was old, made of red brick, in the style of Queen Victoria's reign. The portico was flanked by two columns, the balcony from which Mrs. Folan had stood appearing as any balcony of its size from the century prior would appear. Woosencraft walked with a brisk pace, so much so that it was nearly impossible to keep up with him, the tails of his tailcoat swinging to and fro as he strode forward. When we reached the portico he pointed with his cane to the balcony, saying, "It would not hold a man, not even a small one, look at the railing. I must take a closer look at that. We came to the door, our knocks answered by an employee.

"Good day Miss," said Woosencraft, "I am Mr. Horatio Woosencraft, and this is my associate Professor Theodore Carroll, Mrs. Folan hired us to search this house, now if you could please show me where I may put my hat and coat I would be most delighted."

"Why sir," she said with a start, "Mrs. Folan did not expect you two this early,"

"Early," replied Woosencraft, "Just how early might it be?"

"Half-past three sir."

"Ah yes," Woosencraft said with some laughter in his voice, "I, I must have forgotten to wind my watch up again."

"Well sirs, if you would care to step in, I can take your hats and coats, if you'd like."

"No thank you miss," replied Woosencraft, "I feel it may be a bit frigid within the confines of this house."

"If you please sir," she said, retreating back towards the office.

"Now we'll just be looking through the place, please do not mind us."

She retreated to the office as we ascended the staircase. We stopped on the landing at the place where the footsteps were said to have begun, yet saw nothing. Despite this Woosencraft began to place his feet in the locale, and walked up the stairs, following the path of the footsteps to the balcony, where he stopped just before the railing. He stopped, and pointed at the rot-iron, "Behold Professor, the cuts made into this railing."

"What could they be from?" I asked, adjusting the spectacles I wore on my nose.

"The fingernails of someone, desperately holding onto the railing, only to drop to their death. I think, Professor, we may have much more than a mere tale of ghosts haunting an old home, rather I believe the eternal struggle of Cain and Abel has continued onto this balcony, and that Cain's curse had it's next victim on that day."

"What do you mean, a murder?!"

"Oh yes Professor, but more than that, a gruesome one indeed, the struggle between two persons, separated by their passions, separated by their love for something, a person? Their country? Their King? We may not know now however-"

"However what?" asked Mrs. Folan, approaching from the stairs, what struggle, did the Browne's have some sort of a sorrowful romantic feud?"

"Ah Madam, that was what I planned to ask you. Pray, do tell of the family of Mr. Horace Browne."

"Well, as you well know Mr. Browne was a famed businessman here in Missouri. Years ago, in 1864, the Battle of Westport took place along this very road before us, Browne was a Southern Sympathiser, he even owned slaves at one point. Well one of his sons shouted insults upon a passing Federal company. Now these Yankees were a most cruel sort, they came up to the house and burst through the door, nearly trampling the poor maid to death, they chased Mr. Browne, who had entered the foyer to see what was the fuss, up the stairs and onto the balcony. Once there they forced him atop the railing, and threw him off. Mr. Browne died upon impact. His son, Horace Browne II, took over here and made peace with the Yankees, to ensure that they did not return to haunt his family."

"And pray tell me, Mrs. Folan, just how many ghosts exactly reside at this residence?"Woosencraft inquired.

"The ghosts of Browne the Elder, and Browne the Younger are frequently seen here. However, there are also the ghosts of a pair of young girls, who befell to typhoid many years ago, that can be seen on the grounds of the house. A soldier is also seen, guarding the house from rioters. He oft times will hold me when I am trying to put out the chandelier."

"Yes,"he said, in a distant manner, "I see, yes."

He moved suddenly for the door, spinning around as I followed, he stared with those lonely eyes at Mrs Folan, "We shall return in due course madam. Until then, good day to you."

As we got back into the cab I turned to look at Woosencraft, his eyes were filled with a glee that I have rarely seen since. "Woosencraft,"said I, "where are we going?"

"Ah my dear Professor, that is a mystery to even I right now."

"Wait, so we're in a cab, and its moving, and we haven't given the driver a destination?"

"Exactly that,"he turned to the cabby, "Pershing Street Station if ye please."

We began on our merry way towards the old station, it'd been a century since the grand building had been opened, a century since that fateful year of 1914, when Franz Ferdinand fell to the Serbs, and when the War to End All Wars began. The city passed by us, as we travelled up Main, turning west on Pershing and in front of the marquee where a doorman came to open the cab door for us. Woosencraft led the way into the station, across the granite floors of that marvellous place. I have always admired fine architecture, almost as much as I admire fine music, of men such as Mozart, Beethoven, Bach, and Strauss.

Woosencraft himself was a talented musician, more so than myself. I later found out that he had written three opéras by the time we had met during his second year at Dafydd Sant. I had written an opéra, "Lo Sciocco di Venezia", "The Fool of Venice"it was called. We came to a café, where Woosencraft came to a table, at which none sat.

"Woosencraft, what are we doing here?"I asked, perplexed as it is. "We aren't catching a train are we, they've all left already."

"We are here, my dear fellow, to catch a copyist."

"A copyist,"I said with a start. "What on Earth for?"

"Well if I am to pursue this career I have even less time to make copies of my work. Therefore I am hiring a copyist."

At that point a young woman about our age walked up to the table, "Mæstro?"she asked.

"Ah, Miss Clapham,"Woosencraft said with a smile, "A pleasure to meet you at last. How fares thee?"

"I am well."

"Now, what are your qualifications?"

"I have spent the last four years at the Royal Academy of Music in London sir."

"A soprano I believe?"

"Why, yes sir."

"A pianist?"

"But of course sir."

"A fair cook?"

"I know how to sir."

He stood and began to walk away, tears began to show in Miss Clapham's eyes, Woosencraft, realising what was happening turned, "Worry not my dear," he said to her, "Come to No. 41 Warwick Boulevard tomorrow at 9.00. Come Professor we must be off, Good day miss."

We walked back out of the station, catching another cab, which took us back to Warwick Boulevard. We went into the parlour, where I began questioning my friend, "Woosencraft,"I inquired, "how can we trust this Miss Clapham?"

"Miss Elizabeth Clapham, my dear Carroll, is a woman of dignity, her father was the late Colonel Sir Banastre Clapham, KBE one of Her Majesty's colonial agents, a veteran of the Falklands War. I trust her, as I once trusted a soldier who gave me shelter one dark night when I was in my thirteenth year."

"So you know the Clapham's?"

"I knew them nearly a lifetime ago. Young Elizabeth was a girl of thirteen then. We were the best of friends, I would entertain her with the violin, and she'd respond with her beautiful singing. There were so many arias from everything from 'Rigoletto' to 'Le nozze di Figaro'.

"I was in a hard time then you see, after all my dear mother had just died from typhoid, and I was now orphaned. The Claphams took me in though, and there I stayed, for a year, until Sir Banastre fell ill and died. To be sure I was no strain on their house any longer I left, and came to Dafydd Sant.

"For ten years now I have not laid eyes on young Bethan as we called her. Only now do we meet once more."

He looked at his watch, hanging from his waistcoat, "Oh," exclaimed he, "you'd best be off, have you not a rehearsal of Handel's 'Messiah?'"

"Why, but of course Woosencraft, I'd forgotten."

"Right then, happy conducting to you."

"And good day to you too Woosencraft," I replied, standing and turning to depart, "I shall be back tonight late, with the rehearsal and all."

"Why but of course," my friend replied, "and with Händel one does seem to drag on a bit."

That night as I returned to No. 41 I found the windows on the second floor open, the curtains blowing out in the breeze. As I entered I wondered just what Woosencraft might be up to, having the windows open in December, yet no reason came to mind. I made my way up the stairs, into the room where the piano is kept. As I made my way up the stairs I could hear the most beautiful music coming from the piano, the melody of "The Wren Boys" being played on the treble clef, with the left hand playing a beautiful scale that must have been for a violin or viola.

I entered the chamber, to find Woosencraft sitting at the piano, playing off of one of his scores, he turned when I entered, a score sitting on the piano. "It's done," said he, 'L'Oratorio de Noël' is complete."

"Really!"I shouted in my excitement, "Done! Why Woosencraft, this is amazing."

"Is it Professor?" he said, looking out the window at the softly falling snow.

"Why Woosencraft," I said entering the chamber, sitting in a chair, "You started the Oratorio on the 1st, that's 5 days! Not even Händel could do that."

"That may be, however we must not think on that," he stood from the bench, "rather we must turn our attentions to the matters at hand, the Browne House case. Now what do you make of it Carroll?"

"Well, Mrs Folan says she has seen a ghost jump off a balcony and kill itself. Through this I can deduce she is insane, and this case is just a falsehood, native to her mind."

"Ah, now that's where you, my friend, are mistaken. Yes Mrs Folan is insane, her very nature suggests that. She did, however, see someone depart from that balcony."

"But what?" I interjected.

"That she in fact pushed someone from said balcony,"He declared.

"But who?"I exclaimed, standing.

"That my dear friend," he said with a matter-of-fact tone, "is the question we must ask ourselves. Who,"he held up his index finger, "it was she killed, why,"he held up his middle finger next to his index finger, "she killed whoever it was, and how," he held up his third finger, "she killed the victim."

"But Woosencraft, surely you have thought over this, who could she have possibly killed?"

"Well, say a scandal started and she accidentally murdered the one who started it. Or that she got angry at a volunteer, and threw them off."

"But what if she did?!"I replied in my anguish. My friend turned to the piano and began playing Beethoven's "Moonlight Sonata."

"You'd best get some sleep Professor,"he said, "We've a busy day tomorrow,"and with that I left him to his music, his refuge from "Terra Vera"as we called the real world, and into "Terra Musica,"where his only peace lay in those days.

Morning came quickly, Woosencraft was early to rise yet again. At exactly 9.00 Miss Clapham, appearing to be ready for work, came to call. Woosencraft led her into the music room like any gentleman, and gave her the score of the

"L'Oratorio". She worked for the entire day on it, not coming down until she had completed the first hundred pages. Woosencraft took her work, a gentle smile upon his face. "Pardon, Bethan, would you care to join me at the Municipal Opéra tonight?

'La Bohemé' is being performed tonight, I hear a wonderful soprano is to be singing."

"Why, Horatio,"she said, "I'd love to join you."

"Very well then, at Half-past 7. I'll be coming to call."

"Why, 'tis most delightful good sir. Please come to my flat, I have a number of rooms at Gregory and Oak."

"'Tis there I shall be, my dear,"he replied with a bow. Now I know not when they got back onto given name standings with each other, but I did know that something was to begin, once more, between the old friends. Woosencraft turned to me, "Shall you be joining us Professor?"

"I am afraid not, I have business elsewhere tonight,"I replied, bowing as I said it. I walked up the stairs, leaving the couple be for the evening.

~

Now as you already know, I knew the Honourable Miss Elizabeth Clapham from my youth. I was thirteen years of age when I first made my way to the Clapham estate, and in my fourteenth year when I departed from their kind hands. Those years were some of the best of my childhood, only surpassed by those spent with my father prior to his own unfortunate death.

We were a perfect duo, performing for guests at the house. I was their composer-in-residence for that year, despite only being a young boy of thirteen years. I would play the violin, or piano, and she would sing in her lofty Soprano voice. In those days music was my life, for my own home life had been ripped from me by the sorrow of my father's demise, and my mother's illness.

That evening as we sat in the cab, on the way to the Lyric, we reminisced on those long departed days, when we would play Blind Man's Bluff in the sprawling gardens, and sometimes walk into the hills and valleys of our homeland. She told me of how her mother had lived to see her daughter achieve her dream of performing at Covent Garden, yet had fallen ill to a cancer of the lungs, a result of her many years of smoking, and died a week after her daughter's premiere on the same stage where Pavarotti got his fame.

"La Bohemé" was a grand performance, yet I felt nervous, the reminder of my mother's death to typhoid back in the year 2005 only made my fears worsen. I had lost all my family, all that I had loved from my early childhood. Was I to secure the fate of my best friend from those years. Was I a curse to those whom I loved? And what of Professor Carroll? I did not love him like I loved Bethan, or like I loved my family, yet he was still the closest friend I had had in recent years. The one who had stood by me at Dafydd Sant, the Attorney General's son.

As the curtain fell, we departed from the Lyric, I took her back to her rooms, and then returned to No. 41. When I returned to the house, the lights were on, I headed up the stairs to Carroll's chamber.

~

Woosencraft entered, his opéra scarf still wrapped about his neck. The finely dressed gentleman appeared to be nervous, yet he still had his demeanour about him. "Enjoyable evening Woosencraft?"I asked.

"Quite,"was his reply. "Miss Clapham has enjoyed herself rather nicely. We poke strongly of the past, and little of the present."

"Ah ha!"I said, clapping my hands together as I said it.

"Professor,"he said, "You must realise you are taking this in an odd manner, are you unwell?"

"Unwell?! Woosencraft, I can tell you have feelings for this Miss Clapham. Why not admit that?"

"Because it is not of great importance right now. Now we must focus on the Browne House problem."

"Well, we've deduced that she threw someone off the balcony, but not who, why, or how."

"Might she have been trying to cover something up by coming to us? What do you think Professor?"

"Quite possible."

"But what?"he said, the sound of his annoyance in his voice.

"Perhaps..."I said, thinking. I then shouted, "Woosencraft! What if her husband didn't die in a hunting trip in Scotland?!"

He stared at me, his eyes widened. Woosencraft jumped up from his chair and ran from the chamber, I followed, grabbing my hat and coat. We jumped into a cab that was at the corner of 47th and Warwick.

Arriving at 67th we jumped from the cab, throwing our fee at the cabby. Woosencraft ran into the house, nearly running into a midnight tour group. The women of the tour screamed in surprise, thinking they'd seen a ghost.

"Mr. Woosencraft!" shouted Mrs Folan, "Just what has brought about this intrusion?"

"Pray do tell Madam, of where your husband died?"

"Why, in Scotland! I've told you before."

"And just where is the body?"

"Buried sir! In Fort William!"

"Has this tour gone to the cellar?"

"Mr Woosencraft,"she said sternly, "We do not take our tours into the cellars."

"This one you do," he said pointing his cane at the woman.

She opened the cellar door, a stench of something rotting erupted from the sub-terrain chamber. Woosencraft shined a light into the dark hole. A man's body lay in the cellar, blood stains on his hands.

It was in that manner that Mr. Horatio Woosencraft detained the murderess, Madam Folan. She had thrown her husband from the balcony in a rage. I later discovered that she got the Scottish papers, and had found that a man who went by the name William Folan, her husband's name, had died in Scotland. It was a perfect plan, had the problem of her own mental instability not come to be a factor. For weeks later Woosencraft was a name about the city, his good times only increased with his relationship with Bethan. It seemed the good times could not end.

The Manor on the Moor

The year of 2023 was a most surprising one, of a sickening nature no doubt, but surprising all the same. I had been living at No. 43 for some time now, and had often wondered just what drove my friend to the findings of his person. The stories about his exploits had circulated throughout the salons and clubs of the high society, and the pubs, which we were known to frequent. It was in June of that year that I chose to take a short holiday to my family's manor just outside of the village of Weston, where I had been born and educated up until my years at Dafydd Sant.

During this, venture, I came across the most extraordinary of circumstances concerning my now departed father, the Honourable Justice Ignatius Carroll. At the time he was in his ninetieth year, growing old in the grand home he built many years prior. He was a veteran of the First Iraqi War, once a state senator, and even ran for governor. The great man had seemed unstoppable, if only for a while. Yet when he retired to the quiet life of a country gentleman a decade before he seemed exhausted, as though the efforts involved in his political career had brought him down, panting as though having run the Marathon.

Now I returned to Warwick Boulevard after a week to find the window open, a violin playing Mozart from inside the house. Entering the chamber from hence the sound came I found that my friend Woosencraft was entertaining. He continued to play the merry piece, a grand smile on his pale face, the sound lighter than air, as though not contaminated by the sin that fills this Earth. In an armchair opposite from him sat Bethan, listening intently, as he finished the piece she'd shout, "Bravo, Mæstro." Woosencraft turned, looked at me with joy in his face, "Ah Professor, how good to see you! I trust your venture into the countryside was profitable?"

"Ah but of course Woosencraft," I said, turning now to Bethan, "I trust you've made sure he's been keeping himself well?"

"Of course Professor, you know as well as I do that society as a whole would greatly suffer at the loss of such a marvellous figure," she said with a laugh, then turning to Woosencraft she said, "Oh Horatio! Please tell the Professor the good news!"
"News," said I, my interest now perked, "what could possibly be new with old Horatio Woosencraft?"

"We're to be married professor," Woosencraft said, his eyes bright with happiness and excitement.

"Married!" I exclaimed, "That's grand news, congratulations Bethan, Horatio, grand news. When is it to be?"

"My dear fellow, why the hurry, in the next month it shall be done."

"And to think of it, I've dreamt of it for years," Bethan said dreamily, "The Honourable Madam Elizabeth Clapham Woosencraft, wife to the greatest Welsh composer who ever lived."

"Ah yes, and speaking on the subject how is your Christmas Oratorio coming along then?" I said in an acute manner.

"It is making progress," he replied in a rather bored manner.

"I personally think you should include a chorus of sheep in it," said Bethan with a laugh.

"I know, but this is to start off my career as a composer of the oratorio, I can't have a flock of sheep just walk into my Christmas special, it'd be baaaad. The sheep are supposed to be in the field and get woken up by a group of drunken angels who are singing their way out of the greatest pub in the world, Heaven."

We began to laugh.

"Why not perform for us your Minuet in C Major."

"What a startling proposition my dear Professor," he said, sitting down at the piano, "and one so correct in stating."

He began to play, the hands moving in a beautiful dance upon the keys, playing the beautiful melody with the light airy nature of a dove, and the harmony with the forceful nature of a man of war. The beauty of the allegro was unlike any other. Bethan stared transfixed upon the fingers of the mæstro, how they moved like God's own fingers do to stir the winds to move the seas. I looked at his face, the pale placid face, calm, eyes closed, a look of serene peace quite rare to those sharp features. Those very features began to smoothen, began to calm, he seemed like a young child, a babe just come from the womb, sleeping softly upon it's mother's bosom. The largo was slow, dreamy, like the minuet from Händel's Water Music Suite. It flowed like silk curtains, billowing in a soft breeze, then picking up its swinging nature, a melodic spring rain, light in the upper register of the piano, yet heavy in the lower register. The largo ended like the day of a young child would, when the child's mother tucks him into bed and kisses him on the forehead, then putting out the candle that lights his bedchamber and leaving him to his dreams. The final allegro was like a dream, the tension of the piece rising and falling in a fast motion.

The darkness of the most horrid nightmare, the brilliant glory of the happiest dream. The snow softly falling upon the couple as they kissed beneath the great stained glass of the Church, outside it's glorious doors. He wore his best suit, she her best dress, white in colour a brilliant blend to that day of snow. I watched as Woosencraft and Bethan got into the back of one of my student's cars, so happy were they, on this their wedding day. And yet it seemed not to be Woosencraft, but I who got into the car, another woman other than Bethan taking her own place. We drove off, to No. 34, where we found the door kicked in, and Woosencraft lying in a pool of blood on the floor, his revolver in his hand, eyes wide, saying, "My dear Professor, I have failed." He lay in my arms and died.

"Theodore, Theodore," I heard the voice from somewhat of a distance, a kind face looked down upon my own, "Professor Carroll are you alright?"

"W-what happened?" I asked, in a daze.

"You fell asleep and out of your chair," Bethan answered, her caring face looking down on me.

"Oh, um," I said with a start, sitting up and straightening my necktie,

"Sorry Woosencraft, didn't mean to fall asleep during your minuet."

"My dear fellow," he said, "there is no need to be sorry for it, you've had a long journey. Why don't you go up to bed for a while?"

"Your probably right," I said, standing and exiting the chamber I went down the corridor to my chamber.

I entered, removed my shoes and coat, and lay down on the bed, letting the light of the winter afternoon creep in over my face. The light soon began to fade, my eyes shutting, sleep creeping over me, the exhaustion of the day overwhelming my being.

The corridor was darkened, an old fashioned wood panelled corridor the likes to be found in a manour in the English countryside. I travelled down that corridor, passing portraits of men from centuries past, and of those still alive in the present. As I came to a set of double doors I could hear some sound, a cry of some endangered soul somewhere deep in the place. I wrenched open the double doors, and found a familiar sight, my old nursery from when I was a babe. Yet a man was kneeling at the window, crying out in the pain of his soul, the fear that enveloped him. The man was old, his hair pure white, his hands shook terribly. He turned to face me, the look of fear was great in his eyes, the whites of which enveloped the black pupils. They were bloodshot, fearful. My father opened his mouth and let out a terrifying scream, one that would wake the dead. The scream of the banshee enveloping the chamber. As he screamed I watched his body crumple onto the floor, the body rot until there was only bones left. Then the bones began to rot as well, till only the dust of my father's bones remained.

I awoke with a start, the dream had seemed so real to me that I feared for my father's life. Woosencraft stood over me, my chamber telephone in hand, "a man from your father's manor is on the phone Professor," he said in a matter of fact tone that allowed some sorrow escape.

I took the telephone from him, and fearfully said, "This is P-Professor CCar- roll."

"Good Evening Professor," one of my father's servants by the name of Wylkins said.

"What can I help you with Mr. Wylkins?"

"Sir, it is your father," the air seemed to get twenty degrees colder, "I am afraid he is bedridden. Professor, he is dying."

I dropped the telephone and sat down on the bed. Woosencraft grabbed my shoulder and said, "Well, are you going back up or what?"

"Y-Yes," I stuttered, "I must go. Please tell Mr. Wylkins, for I cannot speak to him right now."

Woosencraft said a few quick words to the butler, and helped me pack. I made the 6.00 train that was headed for St Joseph, yet stopping in Weston. Whilst sitting in the compartment I looked into the window, at the darkness enveloping the night, my own reflection quite clear from the lights from within the train. My face was white, I was shaking with fear, my hands not as still as before. Had it been a prophetic vision? I feared that it was the entire way to the manour. When I entered I found the place dark, the grand foyer only lighted by the chandelier in the centre, the bronze statuary reflecting its golden rays. Mr. Wylkins greeted me at the foot of the stairs.

"Professor," said he bowing, I extended my hand to him, "welcome back home."

"Please Henry," I said to him, "take me to my father."

He led me up the stairs and down the darkened corridor I had seen in my dream. We walked past the pair of double doors that led to the nursery and down another corridor that led from the original one we had travelled. At the end of this corridor we entered my father's chambers. It was an ornate chamber, the dark wood that covered the walls overwhelmed the light that flickered from a candle next to the bed. My Father had been born into a small cottage in the village, growing up with no electrical lights. He had never wanted to install them in the manour house. Thus I had found electricity a new thing when I arrived at Dafydd Sant. He lay in his four poster bed, his face as pale as I had seen in the dream. His hands were wrinkled from old age, the great man now as frail as a babe.

I came close to his bed, my travelling cloak still over my shoulders. I removed the top hat as I reached the four poster, as I came close, setting my candle down on the side table, he looked at me, his eyes frail, as though seeing through some sort of veil, tears in his eyes he said, "Theodore, my son, you've come."

"Yes Father, I'm here, do not worry father, I am here."

"Theodore, I am sorry I cannot stand, however my legs have given indeed."

"Please Father, do not stress yourself," I said, pulling a chair up to his bedside.

"I have missed your music," he said in a quiet manner, "I have missed your beautiful sonatas."

"I swear to thee father, I shall play any sonata you wish, any one, whenever you ask."

"You were always one of the more loyal of your siblings, Augustus merely wants my title, and young Ignatius dreams of only wine, women, and waltzing. Now your sister, she is yet another moral one of our kin, oft staying here with me, keeping me company since your mother's unfortunate death."

He began to sweat, his face pure white with from the strain of speaking. His muscles weak, the piece of thread that holds a man to life straining with the ailments brought about by old age, his demise coming ever closer, the fear of it shone in his bright blue eyes, yet the certainty of it shone as the backdrop of his fear, of his weakness, a foundation for his demeanour, which made certain that he would remain sane, if only whilst that solid form remained.

"Now," he said, with a strained voice, "please leave me to rest."

He turned away from me, the quiet breaths were heavy all the same, his white hair shone bright in that darkened chamber. As he turned I began to hear the rain begin to fall upon the windows that made the French doors leading to a balcony, a soft sorrowful rain, mourning what was coming to pass behind those bleak stone walls.

I left my father's bedchamber, and made my way to my own old chamber, on what seemed a long and never ending walk. The corridors of Athroe House, silent as a crypt, seemed ever foreboding. The dark, wood panelled walls, that had once made a young boy of four fear what lurked from in the shadows, what could come from the darkness of a precipitous night, what banshees or even witches, if they even existed, could spring out from the depths of the night. A dark foreboding feeling that there was no hope left on Earth.

He came to the portrait of Cedric Carroll, the Viscount Fitzconnell, who had lived three hundred years prior. There beside the portrait stood a door, the familiar brass sign reading, Master Theodore made by order from his loving father, many years prior. In those days I had been a young boy, of a mere five years when he had installed the sign, my siblings and I would play out on the lawn, us brothers playing *Cú Chullain and the Hound of*

Cullain, our favourite game at the time. Catherine would play the role of the *cailín* in danger, the damsel in distress. Our heritage was the basis for our lives, we spoke the old Irish tongue rather than English, and for your own benefit I have chosen to translate conversations between my kinsmen and I, spoken in our native tongue, into English.

I entered my chamber, lighting the oil lamps as I entered. It had been left the way it had been the day that I left for Oxford, the wallpaper having not but faded, the wood covered in a slight lair of dust. My shelves of books, of scores and sheet music, still in that form in which I had left them nearly a score of years prior. I had never collected all of my possessions from Athroe, favouring the keeping of them there where they would be safe, locked in this darkened and old chamber.

The chamber was of a fair size, being the third child I did not have the largest bedchamber, that falling to Ignatius who was not only the eldest, but my dear father's namesake. I recalled the day when I sat in that very chamber, the sun shining through the tall windows, as my young face shown with glee that I no longer had to share quarters with Augustus. I had dreamt of a future, a house of my own, a house in the city, where music ruled over all other sensations. I realised then that I had dreamt of No. 43, that I had envisioned that grand life which I now lived years prior to its commencement.

I stretched out onto the bed, having changed into my sleeping clothes, and let my mind wander, to the concert hall where I had first played the piano, where I had first been introduced to the fine music of the baroque masters, Bach, Händel, and Vivalidi. Little did I know that one day I too would help such a master of the art of composition, a little known man, Mr. Horatio Woosencraft.

A bell rang in the house, soon it's vibrations came to my ears. My eyes opened slowly, rising from my bed, I looked at the clock on the wall, noting that it was nine hours past mid-night, I choose to rise and go down to breakfast.

Dressing in my morning coat I headed to the living quarters of the house. From the parlour I could hear a heated argument, "You know that those were sound investments!" a familiar voice shouted.

"Sound?! Sound! Ambidextrous Annie was no sound investment, you lost £ 10,000 on that bloody horse!"

I entered the breakfast chamber to find two men, of great stature standing, faces red. They turned upon hearing my opening of the door. "Ted!" said Augustus, his eyes lighting up upon the sight of his brother.

Ignatius looked less than pleased at my entrance, I presumed it was due to the fact of my success, which neither of them had endeavoured to find. "Ted," he said, a cold air in his voice, "I trust your journey was without trouble?"

"Without trouble yes, without fret for our dear father, no. How long has he been like this?" I asked.

"For the past fortnight he has only become worse, his physician says it is in fact a form of porphyria, yet I worry that he may be falling to the pestilence," replied Ignatius.

"What ever it is," added Augustus, "I doubt he will have to suffer much longer."

"Yet let us not worry about father for the moment," spoke Ignatius with a start, "why not eat, and then prepare ourselves for the tasks ahead."

We sat down at the long table, it's fine polished oak surface, the meal, fine sausage and eggs, seemed dull to the terrible thought, father is dying. After eating I chose to stroll throughout the gardens, recalling the merry games of young children once played within the great hedge maze. A gardener stood along side a hedge about two hundred yards from where I stood. His face was grizzled, a large hooked nose, with wrinkles beneath around the mouth and eyes, from a life of hard work. He wore a dirty rumpled bowler hat, which looked as though it had fallen from its perch too often into freshly sowed soil. I called to him, "Good day sir."

He turned to face me, his eyes were black, familiar, perhaps he had worked for my father when I still resided here. "Good day Professor," he replied, how he knew of my trade I knew not.

"A fine day is it not?" I asked, coming within two paces of him.

"Aye, that it is," he said, his voice grizzled.

"Pardon my asking but, how long have you worked here?"

"A fortnight sir," he said.

"Well, you look like someone I know, did a brother or your father work here before you?"

"No sir," he said, "I've just come over from Wales. I'm attempting to afford my son's education at Dafydd Sant." He smiled, "the school where a modest composer once attended."

"Woosencraft!" I shouted as my friend slowly stood at his full height, "what are you doing here?"

"Oh, I had a feeling that something more than an ailment as befallen your dear father."

"Something m-more?" I stuttered, pulling my handkerchief from my wrist, I felt as though my face were white.

"Oh my dear professor," he said soothingly, "I meant not to frighten you, I only think it is possible, not that it is the fact. But no more of this my good friend, please show me to the gardener's quarters, that I might return to my person."

We strode to the gardener's quarters, where he changed into his usual frock coat, and soon we were walking down the corridors of the house itself. We entered my father's chambers, to find my sister Catherine sitting by my father's bedside.

"Ted," she said with a gasp, then noticing Woosencraft for the first time she said, "I believe we haven't been introduced yet sir."

"My name, Miss Carroll, is Horatio Woosencraft, I am a friend of your brother here."

"Oh, so your the famed Mr Woosencraft!" she exclaimed, standing and curtseying in respect for the honoured man who stood before her. "I've heard so much of you through the papers, they say you have a sixth sense, is it true."

Woosencraft laughed, "Alas milady, I do not have a sixth sense, however some would of course say that is such."

We sat in the chamber, my father still asleep in his bed, his face seemed at peace, despite what terrible ailments had befallen him. I began to ponder the thoughts of his ailments. My brothers had said it was porphyria, an ailment accustomed to the royal houses of Europe. The word brought back memories of my history classes at Dafydd, years ago, of how King George III had gone mad, ill with porphyria. I recalled that it killed him in the end, in 1826, 107 years prior to my own father's birth, it was no wonder now, my father was in his ninetieth decade, he was in his final years.

As I slept that night, my dreams were filled with terrible visions of darkened corridors, wood panelled, with a lone voice crying out. "My God!" it cried, "My God! Forgive your prodigal son!"

I arose from my bed, "Forgive me LORD!" the cries were from some distant chamber in the great house. "Forgive your servant!" I put on a robe, over my nightshirt, "Forgive! Oh LORD! Forgive me!" I grabbed a candle, and ran out my chamber, down the corridors. The corridor was darkened, an old fashioned wood panelled corridor the likes to be found in a manour in the English countryside. I travelled down that corridor, passing portraits of men from centuries past, and of those still alive in the present. As I came to a set of double doors I could hear some sound, a cry of some endangered soul somewhere deep in the place. I wrenched open the double doors, and found a familiar sight, my old nursery from when I was a babe. Yet a man was kneeling at the window, crying out in the pain of his soul, the fear that enveloped him. The man was old, his hair pure white, his hands shook terribly. He turned to face me, the look of fear was great in his eyes, the whites of which enveloped the black pupils. They were bloodshot, fearful. My father opened his mouth and let out a terrifying scream, one that would wake the dead. The scream of the banshee enveloping the chamber. As he screamed I watched his body crumple onto the floor, as he began to gag. My father began to vomit blood, his white night shirt now stained red.

"Father! Father!" I screamed, Catherine ran into the nursery, she gasped at the sight. Augustus and Ignatius followed her, Augustus and I grabbed father's wrists and ankles and carried him back to his chamber. Woosencraft met us there,

"Professor," he said, "what's happened?"

"It's father," I stuttered, "He, he's gone mad!"

"Set him down," Woosencraft ordered, "onto the bed."

We laid him in the bed as instructed, Woosencraft felt his pulse in his wrist, he turned to me, face white, "He's near death, I'm sorry Theodore."

I felt the tears begin to roll down my cheeks, Catherine began to sob, Augustus fell to his knees, Ignatius stood still, face pure white. My father spoke,

"Theodore, Augustus, Ignatius, Catherine, one of you imposed this ailment upon me," he sighed, "and I forgive that one of my children."

He took his breaths with some effort, then he reached towards heaven, his hand falling, steadily, like the falling of the cries of the banshee upon the countryside, his eyes became still, his chest ceased to rise, my father ceased to live.

The chamber was silent, we remained where we were not moving, Catherine silently wept, I closed my father's eyes for the last time. I soon heard a movement from behind me, turning I saw Ignatius walking towards the French doors leading onto the balcony. He walked onto the balcony, turned and shouted,

"Forgive me LORD! My Father, my God!" then he threw himself over the railing, falling to his death below.

I stayed at home for the funeral, departing for Kansas City two weeks after that fateful night. A week after returning to Kansas City there was a time for celebration.

The darkness of the most horrid nightmare, the brilliant glory of the happiest dream. The snow softly falling upon the couple as they kissed beneath the great stained glass of the Church, outside it's glorious doors. He wore his best suit, she her best dress, white in colour a brilliant blend to that day of snow. I watched as Woosencraft and Bethan got into the back of one of my student's cars, so happy were they, on this their wedding day. And yet it seemed the events of that month contrasted each other more than any other month in history, but for that one day happiness overwhelmed the sorrow. They drove off, to No. 34, where I joined them a half-hour later, entering I found Woosencraft standing with Bethan in in the drawing room, getting a glass of wine I raised it saying, "To Mr and Mrs Horatio Woosencraft the Baronet Clapham, long may they live in happiness!"

The Old English Affair

I have oft heard of those places, hidden to the world, locales unknown to man. Such was my excitement when to my residence at No 34 came a love struck young aristocrat. It was late in the year, just after the 105th anniversary of the great Armistice of 1918, when, just as Woosencraft was beginning the second acte of his greatest composition yet, *Les Mystères de la Vie et de la Mort* a French opera for a cast of 1000, to last 1000 hours. The man rushed past Bethan, who with some disgust at the snow now tracked into her parlour began muttering curses and what not at the intruder.

"Baronet Clapham!" he exclaimed in an accent that sounded rather Germanic, then recovering his demeanour he sighed, saying, "Forgive me for this… intrusion, however I believe it was necessary to achieve the proper results." The man wore a scarf over his face, he stood before the window through which a radiant light shone.

"Pardon me *Dorby Panie*[2] but would you care to reveal yourself, *w swoim ojczystym języku.*[3]

"*w swoim ojczystym języku ?!*"[4] asked the gentleman.

"Why but of course!" replied the composer, a broad smile across his pale face.

"Very well then Sir, my ruse is up!" and with a dramatic gesture he removed the scarf from his face, "My name is Casmir Stanisław Wadowiceitz I am the Count of Wadowice."

---

[2] "Good Sir" in Polish.
[3] "In your native tongue" in Polish.
[4] "Thy speaks Polish?!"

"And tell us, lordship, what brings you to call upon us?"

The Count turned, looking at me with disgust, "What I have to say is for the Baronet's ears alone."

"What you may say before me," Woosencraft said, with a graceful gesture, "you may say before Professor Carroll here. He is in my full confidence."

"Very well then. Understand this is one of my greatest secrets, and sirs I demand that you both swear on the very bones of Saint Stanisław," he showed a ring upon his right hand, a small piece of white bone in the centre where a ruby would normally sit.

"Oh we swear Wadowice, you can take our word."

The Count sighed, he then withdrew the ring and said, "It was many years ago, I was just a boy, living in exile in Sweden that I first met her. She was a beautiful young girl, we met whilst playing on the coast south of Stockholm. My mother, may she rest in peace, had taken me there to recover from an infection of the throat, and 'twas there that I first met Katerinia. She was the daughter of the Austrian Georg von Halstatt, who's own father had been exiled after the Great War. She was walking down the lane with her father, when she decided to run ahead. As she did so she slipped and nearly fell off the rock ledge into the sea below. I rushed forward, catching her, before she could fall.

"My mother recognised her father from some distant past, but this was the present, this was our time. We were soon playing together, the young son of a Polish Count and the daughter of an Austrian Baron. I can still remember playing blind man's bluff in the garden outside my mother's sea cottage, as she and Baron von Halstatt sat inside watching, enjoying the latest news from the World Cup that was taking place at the time here in America. This happened for some time, and a month later she came running down the lane again. I came out to meet her, but instead of the sweat on her brow from the run there were tears.

'What's happened? What's happened?' I asked.

'It's papa,' she replied, 'He's dead.'

"I did not see her again for many years, eventually I took up my studies at Sandhurst, to become an officer of the Horse Guards, until I met her again. I was on a tour of the Tower of London, admiring the beauty of the Crown Jewels when this voice of an Austrian sounded, 'Ah they are true beauty are they not your Lordship?'

"I left Sandhurst that day, and we made plans to be married. After our wedding at Westminster Cathedral we decided to come to a convent along the Mississippi in Northern Iowa for our honeymoon. Yet it was there that she disappeared. I panicked, where could Katerinia have gone? I began searching for her, and my best guess is that she came here, or rather to a village near here. Kidnapped, by someone unknown."

His tale at an end he made a sigh of desperation, "Oh Katerinia my love! Oh where hath thou gone?"

"And she is a woman of luxury?" I asked soothingly.

The Count turned to me, teary eyed, "She has a modest wealth, however most of it was mostly stolen by the Socialists and Revolutionaries after the abdication of Emperor Charles."

"I see, and tell us Count, is there any possibility in your mind that she may have already reached her demise?" Woosencraft asked.

He let out a cry of sorrow, "How can you even say such a thing Baronet Clapham?"

"If you would refrain from my noble title it would be preferred, I would rather you used my real name Mr Woosencraft."

The Count showed annoyance at Woosencraft's lack of interest in noble titles, yet being a man of honour he went by his host's demands. Woosencraft now appearing as bored as if he were watching a film produced by the American Red Cross, yet I could tell that beneath the mask of boredom lay a man listening to every word.

"Mr Woosencraft, if you could just begin a search for her, I would be most grateful."

"I can assure you that my colleague and I shall take every measure possible to find your wife," I replied.

"How, if I may ask, do you know she is somewhere near here?" asked Woosencraft.

"B-because of this," he withdrew a piece of paper from his coat pocket.

He handed the paper to Woosencraft who studied it closely. "What do you think Professor," he said, handing it to me.

I looked closely, the paper appeared to have been put under water. It was written in ink, blue ink to be precise. The message was in a code:

edcierrÆainretakÆsnúdÆ

cippanhammÆgebíecnan

"Well, I do not know to tell you the truth," I replied, puzzled at the code.

"I too am uncertain as to it's meaning," said the Count.

"Were there any other messages?" Woosencraft asked.

"Yes, there was one other," he said, pulling another piece of paper from his pocket.

Woosencraft looked at it for a moment, passing it to me next, it too was written in the same code:

forhwonðanÆuncÆneÆgegéanþinged

"This is certainly peculiar," I said, puzzled at the messages.

"Count, we shall send word to you as soon as we have found any evidence," interrupted Woosencraft, rising, he added, "Where can we contact you?"

"At the Hotel Matthews," he replied, rising, he bowed to Woosencraft, and then to myself. I showed the gentleman out, returning to the parlour only a minute later to find Woosencraft having pulled his chalkboard out from a closet, erasing the lists of instruments, and arias in *Les Mystères de la Vie et de la Mort*, and writing the two codes down upon the chalk board.

"Tell me Professor, what is your knowledge of codes?" He asked, without turning to see if I was in the room.

"Well," I replied, I have little knowledge of codes, however the letters do strike me as being odd for an English speaking writer."

"That is true, yet what if the writer is not English speaking," he replied.

"Explain," I said, curiosity filling my senses.

"Take for example the letter 'Æ'. Now this letter is to be commonly found in many archaic tongues, Latin, and Old English for example." He drew dash marks over every "Æ", saying, "This code is such that each Æ equal a space, am I clear Professor?"

"Yes," I replied, "But how do you figure?"

"Because take the formation of the characters used to make the code, they are all letters yes, yet in this form they are not commonly found in any modern tongue except for Icelandic, however 'tis commonly found in Old English."

"So the person who wrote this must know Old English?" I asked.

"Exactly," he replied, "therefore he must be a scholar."

"A scholar indeed," I said, "and if he knows the Countess then he must be of aristocratic or noble birth."

"Precisely," he replied.

"Therefore would he also know Latin?"

"How do you figure?"

"Many scholars who know Old English will have also learned Latin, am I not correct?"

"You may have some truth to that statement. Yet how did you come by it?"

"Almost all European aristocrats learned Latin at some point."

"That is very true," said Bethan, entering, a look of interest upon her face, Woosencraft stood.

"Bethan my dear," he said, "tell me did your father know Latin?"

"Why yes," she said, "after all he did attend Cambridge, and Eton."

"Can you do a job for us," he asked, "a rather dangerous job?"

"What might that be?" she replied, a teasing look in her face.

"Can you put an advert in the paper for a translator, someone who knows both Latin and Old English?"

"Certainly, but do I send them here?"

"No, you give them Professor Carroll's office number at the university. I want you, Professor, to be the one to greet them."

"Very well," I said, "Yet what good will this do?"

"If we are to root out our kidnapper, then we must discover who he is? You shall tell him to respond in English, yet ask him the following questions in Old English: 'What do you know of a Polish Count?' then 'Wadowiceitz is his name, have you heard it?' Watch his expressions closely, I am certain that you should be able to tell if he is the kidnapper, and if he is, you must ring a buzzer, which will have a man who shall sit just outside your office on a bench follow him. Do you understand?"

"Yes, who will follow him?" I asked.

"I shall," Woosencraft replied.

He began to work on deciphering the code. 'Twas rather simple, noting that 'twas writ in a mere tongue, which despite it's deceased nature was most certainly still prevalent in the mind of the code breaker. He sent me down to a used bookstore, looking for a certain dictionary. Upon my finding of an Englisc Dictionary I immediately took it home.

I entered the room in which Woosencraft was working only to find him sitting in his chair, scratching away at the manuscript paper on which he was writing his opératic work. Without even turning to recognise me he spoke, "I trust you have the dictionary?"

"Yes, it's right here," I said pulling it from a pocket of my coat and placing it upon the table.

"Oh there will be no need for that you see," he motioned towards the code which still lay upon the chalk board. It had been cracked. I inspected it. It read as follows:

edcierrÆainretakÆsnúdÆ
Return Katerinia soon
cippanhammÆgebíecnan
Chippenham beckons.

forhwonðanÆuncÆneÆgegéanþinged
Why you not replied?

"My word?!" I exclaimed, "how on Earth did you solve it?"

"It was rather simple actually," Woosencraft replied with an air of boredom.

"You see the symbol "Æ" as I have already told you signifies a space, well the rest was a simple translation from Old English into Modern English."

"Yes but I thought you did not know any Old English," I replied.

"Come now Professor, am I one to admit defeat so early on? I merely went and looked in my copy of *Beowulf* for the words in the code. After finding them in the text of the epic I simply looked for the translated text and thus deciphered the code."

"Yes, but why make me go out and get this bloody dictionary for you then?"

"Oh well I was sincere then, however I thought you might enjoy some fresh air too," he said with a smile.

"Funny. So what do you think it means by Chippenham?" I asked, "Is that not a town in England?"

"It is actually, what do you make of it?"

"Well perhaps she spent sometime between the childhood at the beach and the meeting at the Tower, but I thought she was Austrian!"

"She is Professor, and yes it does refer to Chippenham in Wiltshire. Actually however it may also refer to a certain gentleman who bears the title of Lord Chippenham, as is the custom in the British Peerage."

"Ah so it could be a possible lover eh?!"

"Exactly, a lover indeed. All we need is an answer to my advert and we should have our man who has undoubtedly followed our happy couple on their honeymoon to America."

~

The advert was put into the paper, and I soon began to spend much time in my office. Only a trickle of people appeared. None of them knew of what I spoke, and they were dismissed.

It was not until one day as the rains fell heavy upon the university that a dark haired man entered. His hair was straight, long, and black. He wore a suit, with a frock coat, and a top hat. "Hwaug ðu cunnan réfan Ásweorfan?" I asked.

He looked startled, "Hwa?" he asked.

"Please reply in English?"

"What?"

"Ác sy Wadowiceitz, gefrǽge duguþ unc?"

"What is it to you?" he asked turning about and walking out of the office. I rang the buzzer, standing and following Woosencraft, who was disguised as a priest.

We walked out of the office building, watching as the man got into a car. We caught a cab, having the driver follow the man, Woosencraft saying, "I'll pay you it all when we get there." I was told to stay behind and contact the Count, we were to go to Union Station and await a further message from Woosencraft that would arrive via telephone at Haberdasher's a fine restaurant in the station.

The Count and I sat in Haberdasher's, having already eaten. I reading the paper, he reading something in Polish. Little of interest was to be found in the paper, just a short bit about a play to be performed at the Gottlieb Theatre at Avila, *King Harold*, written by a certain local Irish playwright who had received some fame for his work. As I reached the end of the article the telephone behind the bar rang, the barman called out, "Is there a Professor Theodore Carroll here at all?"

"I am here," I said, standing.

"A gentleman on the telephone for you sir," he said, handing the
telephone to me.

"Professor," said Woosencraft, the sound of voices from behind him sounded, "Take the train to Leavenworth, I'll meet the pair of you at the station, the train leaves Kansas City in exactly five minutes, hurry!" He hung up. I thanked the barman, gave him a tip of three dollars, and the Count and I departed.

We caught the train, getting a compartment to ourselves, he asked,

"Where are we going?"

"Leavenworth," I replied.

"Just up the river from here, only about thirty or forty minutes."

"Is she there?"

"I do not know, maybe, Woosencraft will meet us at the station, 'tis all I know."

"Very well."

We arrived at Leavenworth Station at about 8.40, to find Woosencraft standing nearby, reading the paper. I approached him, about to speak, yet he took the incentive, "Welcome to Leavenworth Professor, Count, follow me."

He led us into the vaults of the station, the fine brickwork gave way to sandstone, roughly carved out. "Tunnels for the post," he explained. We passed through the deserted tunnel, passing yet further into the darkness. After sometime we left the light tunnels and entered a darkened one. Woosencraft extracted a torch from his coat pocket and turned it on. We proceeded, the Count saying something about how he hated the dark. After sometime we heard voices, Woosencraft extinguished his torch, and placing it back into his pocket, he extracted a revolver, which he had loaded, and we continued towards the voices.

"Please Edmund, what are you doing?" a woman asked.

"Katerina!" exclaimed the Count.

"Come now Katerina," replied a man's voice, with the cool tone of someone of high aristocratic origins. "'Tis but a jest."

We progressed further, soon there was a light in the distance. Upon reaching the edge of it Woosencraft motioned for us to halt. We listened for a time, the conversation being a monologue by this Edmund.

"I took you from that Pole for good reason, Katerina. You were engaged to me! To me! And now you are married to a Polish Count! Ha! And not to me, you are now the Countess Wadowiceitz and not Lady Chippenham as you should be! Come here, let me kiss you!"

Woosencraft entered the light, and turned, to face the man, revolver drawn, the Count too drew his revolver and pointed it at Lord Chippenham. He stopped, and stood still, Katerina shouted, "Casmir!"

Chippenham drew a pocket pistol, as Woosencraft shouted, "Drop your weapon!"

He did as was commanded, saying, "Who do I have the honour of surrendering to?"

"Horatio Woosencraft, the Baronet Clapham, and you are?"

"My name is Edmund Chippenham, I am the Lord of Chippenham in Wiltshire."

"Yes I am familiar with the geography of England Your Lordship." Katerina ran from Chippenham and embraced with her husband, tears streaming from both of their faces.

"Oh Casmir, I missed you so!"

"Yet do tell us of just how you went about capturing the good Countess," Woosencraft said, moving across the chamber to sit in a chair. "Well, I met Katerina in London you see, at the meeting of the League of Monarchists at the Ritz. We danced together that night, and planned to meet the next day at the Tower."

"And that is where we met," the Count said.

"Yes," replied Chippenham, "that was where you met her. I had met a colleague from the House of Lords and had entered a discussion with him when the two of you met. When I had turned around she was gone, disappeared. I quickly left the Crown Jewels and asked a guard if he had seen her and he said he had, with leave with a man. That night I described the man to my fellows at the Monarchist League and they told me that it had been the two of you who had left together. It broke my heart when I found out you had been married, I loved you Katerina, I still love you, yet you could not love me in return."

"Edmund please," she said sobbing, "I had met Casmir years before, you don't understand, it was in Sweden, I had loved him since childhood, you were just a friend to me, just a friend."

"I followed the two of you from your wedding, to America. To Dubuque, where you were having your honeymoon in a convent. It was there that I entered with the intent of taking you from that man and marrying you myself!"

"Yet she was already married, it's not possible-" I stammered.

"Professor, to this man anything's possible," Woosencraft replied so as no one else could hear.

"I brought you here to Leavenworth, after hearing of these tunnels under the village from a man in a pub in Dubuque. Yet how did you discover of my whereabouts? The advert in the paper?"

"Oh that came from your code sir. The use of the letters ð and Æ together denoted someone who spoke Old English, as you yourself do."

"My father insisted that we spoke it, he said that we must connect with the history of Wiltshire from whence I come."

"Yes I understand," I said, "my father insisted that I speak Irish, the language of his father's homeland."

"I say," said Woosencraft standing, "Carroll, why not put the kettle on, if we are going to be down here for any longer I'm going to need some tea."

"Right then" Chippenham said, finding a kettle and putting it onto a makeshift stovetop that he had built. The steam rose up through a vent in the roof of the cavern, and turning I saw Woosencraft smile.

"Welcome Inspector," he said, "would you care for a cup of tea?" Three policemen entered, one of them in street clothes, the others in uniform.

"No that's quite all right Mr Woosencraft," the one in street clothes replied.

"Professor if I may introduce you to Inspector O'Leary of the Kansas City Police Department. I called him up here on the same train that I called you and the good Count."

"How… how…?" stuttered Chippenham.

"It was the kettle boiling on the stove that signalled them my lord. They were waiting in the public house just above where we now sit, upon seeing the steam coming from the vent they were to come down through a secret entrance behind the bar that I had found. The barman is a friend of mine you see."

Edmund Chippenham's trial was a memorable one. He was given ten years for kidnapping. The Count and Countess returned to Europe, settling down on and estate in Warwickshire in England. They sent us a letter saying that in thanks for Woosencraft and my efforts in reuniting the couple we would be getting a pension of £500 a year each.

I attended the premiere of Woosencraft's opéra. It was amazingly beautiful. The sights, the sounds, 1000 voices, 1000 instruments, 1000 minutes of music. It truly showed me one thing, life is short, you must live it with those you love, and live it well, or you shall be bored out of your mind, just as I, and the rest of the audience, was by the end of Acte Twenty-five.

The Honourable Mr Graves

In all the time that I have lived with the Woosencraft couple I have heard little of Woosencraft's family. Sure I knew that he was orphaned, only to be raised by his father-in-law the Baronet Clapham, before coming to America to start a new life. Yet by the strangest of occurrences he actually began to speak oft of his kin.

"Well there was my uncle Dafydd Terfel, a fine Welsh gent, excellent baritone too. He was the secretary to the British Ambassador to Greece during the War, lovely chap, always hadn't a clue what was going on in his later years. Must have been all the socialists."

"And then there was my great-grandmother, a certain lady known as Morrison, she lived in Aldershot in Hampshire, a good friend of the wife of a certain Colonel Barclay who commanded the Royal Mallows, this was during Victoria's reign."

Yet the most intriguing tale came with a letter. Now I had figured that Woosencraft had no surviving family, however I was soon to be mistaken. A letter arrived in June, as the summer sun seemed to beat down on us rather harshly. It was a thick envelope, sent via air mail, return addressed as follows:

Mr. Thaddeus Woosencraft
No. 20 High Street
Conway, Wales
United Kingdom

"Woosencraft," said I as I brought the letter up to him. "A letter has arrived from a relative."

"If you would allow me an educated guess, Professor," he replied, his back turned. "I take it that the letter is from the wind swept, dreary, fog covered isle of Britain. And that it comes from a certain gentleman of Welsh origin?"

"How on Earth did you know!" I exclaimed.

"Because my dear Professor," he replied, turning towards me, a calm expression upon his face, "My only living relative is my elder brother Thaddeus of Conway in Wales."

"Well that is exactly who it is from," I said throwing the letter to him.

"Gratzi," he replied, smiling.

"So how long has it been since this brother of yours has spoken to you?"

"Just under thirty years, since we parted ways after the death of our dear mother."

He opened the letter, reviewed it with an air of lax amusement. His eyes quickly darted across the lines, a smile quickly showed upon the man's face.

"What do you make of it," he said handing it to me. I took the letter, and was amazed at the fine nature of the hand which had writ such eloquent words.

"Horatio,
It may have not come to your attention yet, Her Majesty's Government
may very well be repelling the inquest of the major news agencies, however I do
not know of the American media.
I have of late been employed by the Foreign Office in London on the
behalf of Lord Bamburgh the Foreign Minister. I cannot divulge into the situation

much more via post for fear of interception, yet what I can tell you is that it is of a
major importance for the European Community and NATO as a whole. Enclosed
is yours and your friend the Professor Carroll's passage to my residence in
Conway.
Hoping all is well, Your brother
Thaddeus Woosencraft, Q. C."

I looked up, surprised to see Woosencraft standing before me, overcoat and hat already draping his slender frame. He looked at me, glaring, "Well Professor are you not coming?"

"So soon?!" I declared indigently, "I haven't even had breakfast!"

"Our train leaves the Station in 50 minutes, now Professor if you would kindly join me on the street in about five minutes…" he left the room, most probably to go and tell Bethan that we were off for a short holiday to Britain. I met him in front of our residence at No. 43 within the desired time. We called a cab and were soon striding across the marble floors of the Station's Grand Hall towards the platforms. After boarding our train destined for Chicago,

I began to question my friend. "What do you think we are being set on?"

"Exactly what I was about to ask you Professor."

"Well, it references the European Community and NATO, so I would suspect it to involve one of the Eastern European sovereignties, the most powerful of which is Russia."

"Exactly what I was thinking Professor."

"How on Earth did you come to that conclusion so quickly?"

"Professor do you actually think that I would have left on this odyssey of ours so soon had I not actually gone over in my head what or who we may be dealing with?"

"Well no, but... the Russians really? Why the Russians?"

"Because Her Majesty's state secrets may very well be quite valuable to the Kremlin's intelligence."

The conductor opened the compartment door, "Tickets please," he said rather bored. Woosencraft hurriedly removed them from his coat pocket,

"Chicago eh? Where you off to?"

"It is neither your business nor your care to know where we are off to," Woosencraft said hotly, then adding a bit of respect he added, "Sir."

"Oh and what do you know of me that it is not MY business Mr..."

"Aelsby, Arthur Aelsby," Woosencraft said, "and what I do know of you is that you are the conductor of this train, a native of somewhere in the Southern region of this country, most likely Alabama, and that you have a knack for
smoking Cuban rolled cigars, not to forgo the fact that you also happen to have only just recently downed a cup of only the finest coffee that our national rail service can provide, followed by a brief stop in the loo before going on your rounds, am I not correct Sir?"

"How the Hell?!" he exclaimed, in shock.

"Well most of it was an educated guess," replied Woosencraft calmly, "yet by your entrance into this compartment 'tis obvious that you are the conductor of this train, by the complexion of your face and the sun burns on your neck I can denote that you are from the Southern climes, by your accent an Alabaman by birth. Your lips are blackened by the smoke and cigar ash found only in those Cuban rolled cigars that one can find at any drug store in Missouri denotes that you smoke said cigars. Finally that your breath smells of coffee, or what they call coffee on these trains, and you appear to have blemished your trousers, forgoing the fact that your fly is not entirely undone, and that now you are on your rounds, however your reaction of shock shows even the slightest observer that 'tis nothing but the truth."

The conductor leaned against the frame of the compartment door, "Amazing sir," he said, inspecting the next to final point of my friend's observations, "Absolutely amazing. Can I buy you a drink?"

"I'm not inclined to drink at this moment, and neither should you, after all you are working are you not?"

"Yeah but..." Woosencraft gave him a stern look, "Oh okay, good day gentlemen," he said returning the tickets to my friend who replaced them in his coat pocket.

"Did you have to?" I asked, returning to my seat.

"I rather enjoy it, amazing the foolish like that."

I laughed, "Foolish? Well he was a fool for certain."

~

We arrived in the city, catching a cab to the airport where we would then fly into London. Of all the cities that I have visited, Chicago has to be the biggest on this side of the Atlantic, amazing in size and scope, covering over 70 miles from north to south and Lord knows how many from east to west. At the terminal as we waited I even tried one of "Chicago's own", a Kosher hot dog that actually tasted better than any in Missouri. As we left and flew over the city itself, and over Lake Michigan, I could not help but wonder just what my friend was thinking, he was returning home for the first time in nearly 30 years, returning to a home that no doubt had been changed by time, to his only surviving family, save Bethan who no doubt was now staring at the hearth thinking of our very destination. To his brother Thaddeus, long since thought dead, and maybe to the source of all his troubles, to his father's murderer, the one who had haunted my poor friend all these years. We were going into the dragon's den, Wales.

~

The train ride up to Conway from London was long and tedious, partly due to our untimely arrival on Sunday morning when each train stopped at each village along the tracks for those who may wish to return to their village of birth for Sunday. We arrived in the old market town at about Two-o'clock in the afternoon, startled by the changes from our most recent surroundings at Euston Station, London. Woosencraft caught a cab who took us to the home of Mr Thaddeus Woosencraft, Q. C. We stopped at the door, my friend seemed tense,

"Are you all right Woosencraft?"

"Yes, let's just get inside."

After being greeted by a maid who led us into the drawing room. I sat on a sofa, whilst Woosencraft paced across the room, impatient, obviously nervous. Suddenly a crash was heard, the sound startled me, I jumped up just as the oak panelling on the wall opposite of me swung open, revealing a man of about Woosencraft's height. He was a few years older than my friend and I, his hair was beginning to turn white. He wore a similar suit to that worn by Woosencraft, a piece of rope in his hand which he held up in the air as though he had just pulled the rope down from some height. "I suppose I should have put in the stairs," he said dusting himself off, "Now gentlemen what can I do to help you?"

Then looking up, at the man who stood before him, a younger image of his own person, his jaw dropped, tears swarmed in the brothers' eyes, "Horatio!!!!" he shouted, then running with a strength that was not expected of a man of his age he embraced his younger brother.

"Thaddeus," Horatio replied, tears swarming down his cheeks, "'tis good to see you after so long."

Thaddeus stepped back, looked his brother up and down, "You look thin, has that wife of yours been lax in her cooking?"

"No, she feeds me more than even our dear mother," he replied laughing,

"I just do not eat it all, our cat's about 25 stone now."

Thaddeus laughed, "Mine's thirty stone."

"Damn!"

"And this must be your friend," Thaddeus said turning to me, he extended his hand, "Thaddeus

Woosencraft, Q. C., a pleasure to meet you Professor."

"Theodore Carroll, Professor of Music, Rockhall University in Kansas City, a pleasure sir."

"Now Horatio," he said in a manner of a merchant-man when speaking of a new and much needed deal, "I have received a number of paycheques from Her Majesty's Foreign Office. They concern a job involving the Kremlin's chief official within Her Majesty's realm -"

"So what you are saying," interrupted my friend, "is that the Russians have attempted to take something which they have no right to under the law."

"Exactly!" Thaddeus replied, "and the rub of the matter," he said rising from his chair with an air of frustration, "is that they've actually gotten the bloody thing!"

"And what is this thing brother?"

"Are you familiar with the present environment politically in the world Horatio?"

"Well I know that things are tense on a number of fronts, but what of it?"

"Dear brother," he began, sweat pursing down his face, "what the Russians have stolen is nothing less than a detailed plan of Britain's missile defence system throughout the realm and her colonies. In short -"

"-The Russians could easily give this away to some other nuclear armed country who could use it as a reason for attacking a colony or even Britain herself."

"Exactly! We are in grave peril Horatio, and that's why I've called you here to investigate."

"Investigate you say," he stood, "My dear brother one may recall the darkness of the last time we met, or rather parted. You went your way to Law

School and I went my own, to the Baronet Clapham, my father-in-law may he rest in peace. You expect me, after THIRTY years of silence between us, to join you on this little escapade of yours?"

"Horatio, my brother, you have seen the world change as it has over these past 30 years, have you not?"

"Yes, I have seen change, *benem et malum*."

"And you Professor, have you seen such change?"

"I would have to say that I have sir."

"Oh please do call me Thaddeus, I am not one for pleasantries. Yet, Professor, have you observed the changes that you have seen?"

"I do not understand, what do you mean by observe?"

"You know that there are a number of nations on the Isle of Britain itself have you not?"

"Yes, England, Wales, Scotland, and Cornwall."

"Yet have you ever thought as to just what that number is?" asked Thaddeus

"Well no, but how is that relevant?"

"Because if one has observed one knows every detail of the question at hand. I asked you of the number of nations on the Isle of Britain and you listed them to me yet you could not tell me just how many nations there were on said Isle off the top of your head, therefore you have not observed."

"How rather -" I began, lost for words.

"Simple?" added my friend.

"Un-embellished?" added Thaddeus.

"Yes, how bloody candid the truth of the matter is!" I exclaimed, laughing.

"Candid indeed Professor," said Thaddeus, then he added, "Would you mind going to the corner there and ringing for the maid? I could use a glass."

"Oh certainly," I said, standing and ringing the bell. Upon the maid entering, Thaddeus, with a stark nature, spoke like a commander of some frigate at Trafalgar or Cape St Vincent, "Molly, three glasses if you please. Oh and bring up a bottle of sherry."

"Yes sir," she said, curtsying as she left.

"Now," interjected my friend, "to business, if you do not object my brother."

"Not at all, I was prepared to make such a statement," replied the elder.

"Great minds oft think alike," I said, beaming at the brothers.

"Matters which one of us your calling great," said Thaddeus indignantly.

The duo laughed, then Thaddeus began, "I have tickets for the pair of you on the late train back to London tonight. You will take this," he handed a sealed envelope, "and give it to the gentleman at the Foreign Office who meets you at the door. He in turn shall take you to the Foreign Minister who will give you a better view of the situation. However tonight, I was wondering if you'd care to come to a local church where a number of Men's choruses and soloists shall be performing everything from that traditional music to the great opératic works of the last three hundred years."

"Yes I believe that would be a delightful event," I said, standing.

"Where are you gentlemen staying at if I may ask?"

"At a local Public House," replied my friend.

"Very well, let us meet here at say 6.00 tonight for the concert," Thaddeus said, standing as he spoke.

"Good day Thaddeus," I said shaking his hand, Woosencraft gave a similar gesture towards his brother, then turn about and led me out of the house.

We returned to the Public House, the place was rather clean, much more so than most similar establishments in America. I was struck by the fact that it was less of a bar and more of a social gathering place for the village. The barman was a nice enough gent, he showed us to our room above the bar, a rather dark, wood panelled place, with much dust covering every available surface. Woosencraft immediately crossed to the window, shutting the curtains and then crossing back to the night-stand he grabbed a box of matches and light a candle which he carried to the side table flanked by a pair of old wing-backs on the opposite side of the chamber, in front of the great hearth which, though at present empty, could have heated a family of 10 in the depths of Winter just by the size of it's cæsium. "One cannot be too careful," he said his back turned from me, "Though Thaddeus is my brother, he is known for attracting some rather, unwanted, company. He has had only 10 to 15 attempts on his life in the past 2 years."

"Yet how would you know that if you haven't even seen him in thirty years?"

"Because I have always kept an eye on him, through a certain contact here in Wales, a gentleman by the rather common name of David Thomas who once served in the home of my father-in-law.

Bethan's the one who started it, hearing from me of how my brother was brilliant as a youth."

"Yes but why draw the curtains?" I asked.

"Because I am most likely not the only one who pays someone to tail the Learned Thaddeus Woosencraft, Q. C. I have not a doubt that nearly every sovereign government of Europe has at least one man in Conwy, so as to watch the great Queen's Counsel. Therefore anyone who should be watching my dear brother's residence should also be watching who enters and leaves. No doubt therefore we were of particular interest, you with your colonial accent, and your questioning me, using my surname, which would have surprised any onlooker who knew my brother in that he would most likely have not acknowledged the existence of his younger brother who he likely took for dead. My brother's lack of prudence in not drawing the curtains that flank that window, out of which such a fine view of the harbour and castle is to be seen, would have made it much easier for any person watching the house to have just gone around the back and into a neighbouring building so as to watch from some nearby window. No doubt what ever spy should seek out my brother's misfortune shall be fluent in English, their native tongue, and lectionis labri."

"Lip reading?!" I exclaimed with some laughter.

"I see your Latin is improving Professor."

"Woosencraft you know very well that I have known Latin since my days of home-schooling under the governess at my father's manour."

"Ah but I merely tease," he said caressingly.

"So, you ready for the concert?" I asked abruptly.

"Oh a concert with the learned Queen's Counsel, what a delight," he said with as much sarcasm as any gentleman of his nature could muster.

"Come now, at least your not going with that lady copper who stands on the corner of Warwick and 41st, always snapping at you for your organ playing."

"Ah yes, She Who Must be Obeyed," he said with an air of dignity, bowing at a dead plant in the corner of the room, covered in enough dust as to have not been cleaned since at least the death of Archduke Franz Frendinand at the hands of the anarchist rebel. Woosencraft stood silent for sometime, looking into the fire, obviously thinking out the case which presented itself to him. I too began to wonder about what awaited us in London.

Finally after sometime he spoke, "The Russians seek something from Britain. We are like the Russians, Professor. Tonight we too seek something from Britain," he turned, and walked to the door, "Come my friend, let us dine on Welsh lamb before joining my brother at the concert hall."

We ate a quick meal, before departing from the public house for the Church of Saint Dwyn. It was an older gothic structre, built during the reign of Edward IV of England. The interior was alight by numerous candles, supported by two rows of candelabras on either side of the nave. In the centre was the high altar, in the old Latin fashion, having not been altered by those changes of Vatican II. As we stood in the back of the church, I began to hear the sounds of rain softly falling upon it's tile roof, and soon heard the roar of the thunder, like the sound a bowling ball makes when it is rolled down an alley. Immeadiatley following, the night sky was alight with a great heavenly fire, which struck down onto the Welsh countryside like a meteor from Heaven. The thunder roared once more, this time from the street outside the church, a strike of lighting outlining a man of great height, his hair facing out in each and every direction. He wore a rumplled top hat, an overcoat drenched in the tears of the angels. His umbrella caught the attention of most in the church, it's end smoked, he looked at it, blowing the fire out he shrugged saying, "The bloody 'brelly must've stuck out in the air!"

"Welcome Thaddeus," my friend said.

"And a fine welcome indeed," he replied with an air of indignation, "I've
just nearly been set alight by the bloody celestial fire!"

"It happens to only the best amongst us."

"Yes, well shall we take our seats?"

We sat, soon the programme began, a piece well known to all of us, an oratorio, *The Life of Saint Peter*, as writ by my very own Horatio Woosencraft. Thaddeus and I sat back in awe, as my friend began to drowse off. It was beautiful. The music softly floated over us all, the angelic voices of the sopranos seemed to levitate 'pon the night air, as the great strong basso section reminded us to remain bound to the hard earth. As the programme came near its conclusion some two hours later the conductor turned to the audience, saying,

"It is not I who you should laud, rather 'tis the composer himself, Mr Horatio Woosencraft!"

My friend stood, bowed, the conductor then called to him, "Mæstro,
would you not wish to join us and sing the final chorus?"

"Very well," Woosencraft said hesitantly.

Now I had never heard my friend sing
before, yet to hear him now was
just awe inspiring. Whilst I would register in the
baritone range he had the full
range of both a Tenore I to a Basso. He stepped
forward, and as his great finale
began, the roar of the brass, and the booming sound
of the bass strings echoing
through out the nave of the church. It was a grand
portrayal of one of his greatest
works ever. The beauty of the entire world, all it's
joyous wonders seemed to be
omitting from this man, this genius, my friend.

~

We departed for London in the morning via
the earliest train possible. Woosencraft feared that
with his performance the night before the Russians
would be onto him in the morning, and so before
first light we departed from Conwy, the beautiful
castle town in North Wales.

Arriving in London near midday
Woosencraft quickly led me through the masses of
people at Euston Station. We hired a cab and drove
to the foreign office at once, not even stopping for
lunch. The street outside the office was a fast paced
thoroughfare, with a mass of pedestrians moving
quickly along the street.

The building itself was a fine Georgian edifice, it's
very presence showing off what was the glory of the
British Empire. We quickly entered through the
main entrance, a man stood at the door. "May I help
you sirs?" he asked politely.

Woosencraft showed him the envelope saying, "Yes you may." He froze, looking at the envelope, then at Woosencraft, and finally at me.

"Very well then sirs, if you will come with me."

He led us up the marble staircase, through darkened corridors of this once
great building. Often men and women would pass us by, walking at a fast pace.
Our guide said hello to each of them, continuing deeper into this great building.

At last we entered the office of the Foreign Minister. It was a fine room,
great in size and spectacular in it's very nature. An elderly man sat in a wing-back chair in front of a fire. "Mr Woosencraft," he said softly, "I'm glad to see
you've come."

"Sir it is an honour," he replied, bowing.

"Please, do not bow," replied the Minister," but sit. I trust this is your
colleague Professor Theodore Carroll?"

"Yes sir," I replied, shaking the Minister's hand.

"Now Woosencraft, what have you gathered on our situation?"

"Besides the facts that it involves the Kremlin, that we are dealing with a
state document of immense importance, and that its entrance into Russian hands
could signal the beginning of another World War, this one involving nuclear
weaponry, I know nothing whatsoever about the case."

"On the contrary Mr Woosencraft you seem to know a great deal. How did you figure?"

"'Tis a minor fact of trivialities sir. Firstly that it involves the Kremlin was
obvious, in that they are the greatest non NATO power is one thing, but that they
are armed with nuclear weaponry is just another commonly known fact. That it
could provoke a World War seemed rather obvious also sir, noting that Israel and
Iran are now at each other's heads, for all we know they could be fighting in the
skies over Arabia any day now."

"Comment exactement corriger Monsieur," said a man who had been
standing in the corner, now coming into the light. Woosencraft stood.

"Gentleman pray do not be alarmed by the presence of -"

"Your French colleague Monsieur de Valions, of the French Embassy in
London."

"Oui Monsieur, and too am I worried of the consequences of these
documents falling into the hands of the Russians! We must protect the West, and
Israel, from Iran or her allies, including Russia, from getting these… documents
of value."

"And where are these documents at present?" I asked.

"They are with a chief member of the Foreign Office, a certain Mr Graves,"
replied the Minister.

"Graves! Ha!" shouted de Valions, "do you not even know your own staff
Minster? Graves frequents the St George Club -"

"Your point Monsieur," replied the Minister with an air of annoyance.""

"The St George is also frequented by the Grand Duke of Russia, and the Russian ambassador as well."

"Where does this Mr Graves reside Minister?" Woosencraft asked, an alarmed look upon his face.

"In Kenley, Surrey," just go to the local Public House, you'll find him there," replied the Minster.

Woosencraft rose, "I believe our business in London is concluded. If you will follow me Professor I believe we can find our way out. Good Day Sirs," he bowed, then left the chamber.

"Good Day," I said, leaving.

"Come Professor!" Woosencraft called to me, "We must depart for Surrey!"

We caught a train, going straight to Kenley, running from the station to the public house. The place seemed like any pastoral establishment. The barman came over to us, "What can I get you gentlemen?"

"A pint of your own brew sir," replied Woosencraft, placing a pound on the bar, "and information on a certain Mr Graves."

"What do you wish to know of Graves?" asked a man of great height and a strong build.

"Ah Mr Graves, I just wished to know where you reside that I may come and search for a certain document of state."

"You aren't going anywhere near my house!"

"So I take it you haven't the documents eh?"

"No of course I haven't the bloody documents!"

"Then who does?"

"Motodov!"

"The Russian ambassador, you bloody traitor!" Woosencraft shouted.

Graves threw a punch at Woosencraft, which he dodged, "You will all see that I
am acting in self defence," Woosencraft said, removing his coat and punching
Graves in the face. He fell to the ground, whimpering. "Bring us to Motodov, or I
swear you will face the full force of the Royal Constabulary!" Woosencraft said
scathingly.

Graves rose, "Very well sir," his face was bloodied from his fall. He
walked out of the Public House. We had a short walk to a small manour nestled
in a glade. We entered the house, it had a simple elegance. He led us into a
second floor bedchamber, where on a desk sat the documents. "Here they are
sir," he said, handing them to Woosencraft, "what will you do to me?"

"Only what I shall do to you Graves," said a voice from behind us in the
doorway. I turned, Motodov stood there, a pocket pistol drawn. "Hand the treaty
to me, sir," he said to Woosencraft.

Woosencraft did as told saying, "Very well sir you win," there was a bang
downstairs, "yet the constabulary shall have the ultimate victory today."

The Russian showed signs of fear, his hand shook, he fired a shot, Graves
crumpled to the ground next to me, his blood splattered upon my shoes. The
constable ran upstairs, detaining the Russian ambassador, returning the treaty to
my friend.

~

"A well done operation I must say," remarked Thaddeus who sat across
from me in the Foreign Minister's office.

"Yes however the death of Mr Graves was rather regrettable," remarked
the Minister, "He was my daughter's fiancée."

"I am very sorry for the loss of your familly," I replied.

"Still at least we have secured the peace," said Thaddeus, standing.

"Life is so precious," said Woosencraft, who sat staring at the fire, "One
second it exists, one second it is no more. We can find the pure beauty of God in
life. His very being is life, and the loss of a life is always a minor result of a
regrettable moment in time."

"Mr Woosencraft," said the Minister standing, "I must thank you for
ridding Her Majesty's government of this situation, Her Majesty herself wishes
you good health and a safe journey home."

"Thank you sir. I think we've had enough of Britain," he turned to me.

"Yes, let's go home."

We rose, and began the long journey home,
back to No. 43, back to Bethan,
far from Whitehall and the ministries of power.

Caffydd

IN THE REIGN OF ALBUS REX DID LIVE TWO FRIENDS,
One a woman of grace, dignity and piety,
Another a man of honour and words.
He did come from
the Ould Ordere of Éireann,
She of a modern variant,
Yet peace was true a'tweene theme.
The laddie, Diarmuidus by name,
was a gentleman,
Who lived on his family's manour
in the West, named Clonroe,
The lassie, Ignatia by name,
was a lady dignified,
Who lived on her family's lands
north of the Great River.
The lad loved the arts,
of which he was a patron.
He would play his harp for her
during those quiet times
When only the birdsong, harp
and whispers of the rose could be heard.
The gleo-beam song
shone over all other song,
The birds danced about the friends
In joy and divine Peace they lived,
fore Amo Deo ruled over all.
They knew no sorrow, no fear, no pain.

Oh the sorrow that befelleth their happy world,
As lo the sun would not arise
through the darke flames of woe
And joy was dormant.
Now Diarmuidus feared what
the night would bring
Yet a coward he was note, fore the
fear hade note consumed his soul.

Alas he was note the strongest of spirits
His heart weak, his resolve strong
The steel-beam not seen
yet for a greater might existed,
Chaffydd the great harp of beauty
sang through the night
The lyre string resounding like
 the belle over the countryside
She could make the Tinebrúide
cringe in its coils,
Its thick hide cringing before beauty
Music gave heroes hope of a good to come
Better than the future trials
to be encountered.

Diarmuidus left Clonroe at dawn
        Riding his faithful mare Nos Don
        Across the moorlands to the south
        To the Pillars of Sancto Petro divine
        Where liveth the dragon Méall
        Did stand guard over the pass
        Which stood between two mounts
        On which a pair of shrines stood
        The east to the Father Lord
        The west to the Son King
        An' through out to the Noafa Sproíde
        Alas desecrated by Méall the dragon.
        Now the true guardian of the shrines
        was the stag Cara
        In chains at the foot of the Shrine
        to the Father
        Where in pain he rested, his mournful song
        echoing off the pass's walls.
        His song was heard by our hero
        Who crossed the moor swiftly to the pass
        that he might free the voice

Yet Méall stood in his way.
She had taken the form o' a beautiful muse
Singing the most gorgeous song
known to Man.
Her seemly features concealed to none,
But to lure him to sleep and devour
the man she plotted.
She sang to Diarmuidus thus:
"O noble lord, art thou tired
from thyne journey?
I have food here for the noblest of men,
And wine greater than any other."
Yet the Champion was resolute,
"I require only that which is good."
Meall responded, "And you shall have it
Yet art thou tired noble Diarmuidus?
Come you may lie in my home,
That a noble hero may receive
his just reward of sleep
Denied to him by God and Man alike."
Diarmuidus hesitated so,
As sudden was his urge for lust,
This woman's beauty consuming his senses
Her words caressing the feelings
of longing within him
Yet as he began to speak, Cara sang:
"Oh hero deny evil its victim,
Come free this noble person
Who is so duly afflicted –"
"Listen not to the wind noble sir!"
Crieth the demon
"Listen to your love so dear,"
He turned, to see Ignatia afore him,
"Come to me, hold me true love!"
"O hero that is not thyne love,
Dear Ignatia lies asleep at home,

'Tis a demon who tormenteth you so!"
Thus sang Cara.
"Be gone demon!" cried the Hero
As he ran for the source of Cara's voice
Where he found the stag chained
Its hide bloodstained
As the sounds of Méall's fury came true
And Diarmuidus learnt to fear.
Then forth with thyne harp noble hero,
And to breaketh the chains of woe
That Cara the Stag may rise up
And to the ground beateth the vile demon
Who stalketh the world for to long.

Then Cara sang to Diarmuidus
      As a father would to his son
      "Those who pass these pillars should know
      That nothing awaits them but death and woe
      But on the other side thou shall see
      A land that is good and free
      From evil's grasp and night's chain
      Lest you give good others pain.
      Six more trials thou shall face
      Six more dungeons without grace
      The first you have passed,
      Lust, man's fall, is in the dust;
      Yet through Gluttony thou shalleth pass
      Then thyne Greed thou shall face.
      Acedia shall trouble you next
      Yet despair shall drive you to madness
      If you should succeed thus far
      Then sloth shall be thyne abar.
      Soon wrath shall overcometh thee
      Followed by envy's fearful spree.
      Your pride shall be a challenge I fear
      Yet if you should pass then

vainglory will cost dear.
Thyne noble companions
Caffydd the Magic Harp,
And Nos Don shall grant you speed.
But should you surviveth peace be your's
Light and life shall return once more
And day shall destroy the night.
But go noble Diarmuidus
Go noble lord
And Godspeed to thee."

As through the pass the Hero went,
Travelling further south
across the Lesser River walked
Then into the lands of Iacobus he spent
Where war hath taken hold
Yet also home to a monastery
'twas said where peace reigneth
Through the river plain rode he
Nos Don carrying him with great speed
Into a great cloud of ash and woe
The flames of Hell consuming
the southern lands
As where no joy to be found
But the cries of fallen
and dying men resoundeth
The countryside a barren wasteland
Bog consuming the floodplains
Where once joyous harvests flourished.
To a turn in the road atop the hills
Where stood a banquet table fulleth
Lords of War and slaves alike feasting
If not in seeming joy as in hunting
For the men were rounding in shape
Their faces red, full of meat and mead
Served by fair maids of the northern climes

"O women," said he,
"they shalleth be the death of me."
Then one of the feasters saw him and said
"Behold another to join our merriment!
Come good sir and join us is food and drink
That you might sing of
your travels to we the weak."
Diarmuidus was tempted by the food
For he had not eaten all day
Yet he feared he might lose his way
Alas still the smells of the chicken,
rice, and bread consumed him
His every urge to eat and devour them
For no dish had yet been known to man
As this delicacy of the
feasting table at Athbán.
A voice not his own then spoke softly,
"Well one morsel shan't do any lad harm…"
Under the pow'r of the witches he became
As he made to sit and fast all day
But through the barrow as soft as snow
A rack was seen hurtling thro'
And Cara appeared charging the table
Crying to the witches "Leave the man be!
He is greater than any of thee
My form is gone
My race may be run
But there is still life in me!"
They hissed and catcalled the stag
Crying out like the banshee's on the wind,
"Noble Cara you fool!
Why return after what we did to you?
Now dance with us and sing
To our lord and master,
The devil king!"
They began to dance,

As the drone of a fearful pipe start'd
And the table emptied as the
maid witches danced
The Lords of War and slaves
dancing with thee
Yet Diarmuidus had come around
And forcing his way into
the centre of the circle he found Cara
Trapped by the vile merriment
The gluttonous men and
fearful witches encircling him.
"Diarmuidus the harp!
Let Caffydd sing!" cried the stag.
Quick as a flash the lad
brought the harp from his back
And began to play a merry tune.
The pipes began to squak and splutter
As the witches soon began to flutter
As though lifted from
the ground by some invisible man.
Then the feasters smiling,
regained consciousness
And through the circle came
a feeling of joy and bliss
Royally Cara stood, proclaiming this song:
"Horrid women of Athbán leave these men,
Thou hath no right to them
They are free as God intended
Now be gone demons from this land!"
And as he sang the witches fled,
Running in all directions
Some taking flight,
Sprouting great black wings
like those of a bat,
And forth to their master in Hell they went,
Telling of their foe on Earth.

Now up the crag the noble one made,
      His aim to be free of that place
      And through the brambles of many a bush
      Where all he wished to do was push
      For his horse refused to go further
      When caught in little more than a sewer
      As the flow from the hills
      above came down 'pon the road.
      Diarmuidus though sore
      and tired chose to move forth
      Yet soon his very being felt a need to rest
      And to an inn nearby made his best
      Where a man of portly nature
      Stout face, fine beard,
      and rounders for a middle
      Did greet him at the door.
      "Ach goodly sir what brings ye here?"
      cried the keeper.
      "I come sir looking for a bed
      and perhaps a meal,
      Lest I fall 'pon my weary way
      all to Dúngeille;
      So please forthweth I ask of thee
      To allow this rover to stay.
      "Of course lad!" cried his host
      Who took the horse's reigns with a boast
      "I've kept inns from Ard Macha
      to Contae Mac Eoin,
      Yet ne'er hosted a lad of thyne stature."
      'Twas so that the goodly host
      gave our lad a fine feast
      The brew was fine, the tarts sweet
      The two lads laughed the hours away
      'till near the moon's highest the Hero said,
      "Good host I thank thee!

Yet tell me what is thy name?
I beg to know, as a man
wishing for knowledge."
"My name is it ye want?
My name it is you'll have:
Ralph mac Arnulf is my name,
Bombast and bumbler is my trade
Carrying carrots and crowns
for serfs and kings alike
I will ne'er put out the light
Of joy and happiness
Yet of sorrow I know nothing
And care e'en less.
So if thou shalleth mindeth me
Care not for I shan't scream,
I know nothing of such nonsense
And only of wine, women and song
So let us go for another drink!"

THEN PAST THE CROSSING
    AND TOW'RDS MIGHTY DÚN BÁS A FHÁIL
Where many a lesser man
would have fallen to temptation
Consumed in the fires of
the vile land below the Earth,
Where the Prince of Demons
had his domain.
Diarmuidus strode forth
with Ignatia hand in hand
With Caffydd strapped to his back,
Towards the Cave Entrance,
where no living man had yet enter'd.
There a dim spirit of a man met the lovers:
"Who cometh to the Fallen One's door?"

"'tis I, Diarmuidus, servant of the LORD
GOD,
Cometh to thyne hall,
That I might seeketh the light
on the far side of thyne land."
Now the fame of the great hero had spread
far across the many lands of Earth
And here too in Dorcha's realm
his name was known,
Diarmuidus the Strong of Heart,
Diarmuidus the Wise,
Diarmuidus the Bard of beautiful music.
'twas so that the gatekeeper Daor,
welcomer of those who should pass
Into lands unknown to the sacred and pious;
Did stare with amazement at the noble hero
who stood before him.
"But thou hast not been condemnedeth for
such a crime!
Why doth thou wish to enter this land of
darkness?"
"I wish to seek out the vile weed at its roots,
That it be torn out where
't weakens its own self."
Daor knew not what to say,
for his master had taken his thought.
Then a great voice, cold in its very nature,
That sent a shiver of fear down the spines of
the lovers did commandeth his slave,
"Let them come! The lord of this land
wisheth to great his guests."
"If that were not the feared
Tiarna Dorchadais,
I knoweth not who should have
such a voice as that!"
"That voice maketh me feel o so afraid,

So that I should worry greatly of what
shalleth become of our love
Lest we stray far from that fearful land,
which lieth before us," cried Ignatia.
She shook from head to toe, her face the
palest of white.
"Do not fear my love," Diarmuidus replied,
with growing strength
He drew Caffydd from his rest upon
the back of the bard,
Then to play quite a merry tune, as not heard
in Hell for many an age,
The *Salve* and *Protoevangelium* he chanted
as they descended further and further
into the fiery depths:
"I will put enmity between you and
the woman,
And between your offspring and hers;
He will strike at your head,
While you strike at his heel."
The chant was heard all throughout the
realm of Dorchadais
It echoed off the cavern walls, and through
the dark woodlands
They crossed the River Dóilteáin,
Within whom floweth the blood of millions
Whose hate, envy, and wrath consumeth the
fire that once burnteth there.
There on the opposite bank
he saweth many accursed ones,
Condemned to live on the other side
of the Dóilteáin;
There on the bank opposite
stood many guards,
They had once been human,
once many years ago,

Yet twisted by the wickedness
of their souls they had become
Worse than the accursed.
Their God given beauty had vanisheth,
Just as their morality had,
o so many years ago.
Diarmuidus beheld the sight of these beings,
Not human, nor demon, but in between.
They were the coloureth a dark red,
A blood red, yet a tint of white and gold
shoneth through
For once they had been
Angels of the Heavenly Host
Only to fall with Dorchadais to their doom.
Now Biotáille dorcha, they stood artificial.
They stood bare, their bodies emmiting a
faint glow,
Each bore a tail coming from their anus,
It curved about their bodies, a great spike
perched upon the tip.
Some of the accursed attempted to make it
to the river's bank,
Yet the Biotáille Dorcha forced the wretched
back to the crowd.
Here liveth the worst of humanity,
Now they sorroweth like those they had
harmeth in life.
Diarmuidus called for a boat, yet none came,
"We carry not the living and blest across
Dóilteáin!" cried the boatman.
"Behold, the power of Our Lord God!"
shouted the bard,
He held Caffydd high beforeeth his person,
Then to pluck a string
he found it a challenge,

For many a vile being sent curses reigning
down upon the noble harp,
That it should cease to play its merry piece.
Yet too from his shoulder pouch came a
Holy piece,
For here was the Holy Crucifux of Our Lord.
He held it high before him, with Ignatia in
this other hand,
As the harp played merrily before him, as
though carried by an angel.
The Biotáille Dorcha could not look directly
at the Cross
But cowereth down
at the sight of the Holy item.
The lovers floated across the Dóilteáin,
Landing safely onto the other bank.
There he cried out so all could hear:
"God loveth all thee so!
His son hath dieeth for thyne soul!
Remember that his love remains true
Despite thyne enslavement
to this shore's rue.
Now the souls of the accursed seemed lifted,
Yet they still remained
in bondage as e'er before.
Then to the road leading to Dorchadais' hall,
Where 'twas said many
had been known to fall.

**'TWAS THERE IN THE HALL THEY WERE MADE
KNOWN,**
As through all the day and night
they had scarce to be shone.
Then to enter they did,
and what a sight indeed.
As the many heads of

the feasters turned to behold the arrivals,
For there Diarmuidus
and Ignatia stood proud,
The Holy Crucifux raised on high.
And at the high table they saw,
A man sateth there,
His features like a masque of thin velvet.
The wings coming
from within his back were blacken'd
By the many ages
in which he had dwelt in damnation.
Behold o learned reader and list
For hear sateth Dorchadais,
the Prince of Demons himself,
Before noble Diarmuidus,
and fair Ignatia at the hero's side.
"Welcome noble bard, to my fine hall," he
said, in that fearful voice.
"I come, Dorchadais,
to demand the Light be restored to Earth!"
proclaimeth the hero.
"Ah but 't is not mine to give,"
chided the dark one.
"Ne'er is it your's to take!"
 shouted our hero.
"Ah, but why confront me, noble sir,
For to dine I beg of thee!"
"I shall eat from no table
but the Lord God's."
"Then perhaps a fine body for thee,"
called the fallen one,
He motioneth towards the many accursed
men and women who lay there about him.
"They're mine you know," he said,
"sold their selves to me."
"I shalleth never sleep with a woman

save my wife!"
"But I give this one to you
as a wedding gift, Diarmuidus,"
laughed the vile one.
His laugh was a hard one, a cold one.
Cold as iron it rang in the hero's ears,
Then the fallen one came down
from his dark throne,
Came to Ignatia's side,
"I takeeth thee for my wife," he said.
Then as he made to kiss the poor woman
she rebounded against him.
Drawing from Diarmuidus' haversack
she took,
The Holy Crucifux, which she held
before the dark one.
He fell before it,
unable to stand the sight of it,
Then her heel cameth down upon his head,
As the vile one attempted
to change into many forms.
First as a serpent, then a stag,
Then a wild boar, and a fish of the sea,
Next a fair maiden,
finally back into his proper form,
When he heard those words again:
"I will put enmity
between you and the woman,
And between your offspring and hers;
He will strike at your head,
While you strike at his heel," this time
spaketh by Ignatia herself.
She appeared alive and alight,
as her lover Diarmuidus
and she shone their grace about the hall.
Then consigned to flames of woe,

the dragon cried, "Taketh what
thoust want woman!
Leaveth me to my peace!"
"Thou shalt ne'er have peace,
vile rebel 'gainst Our Lord above!
Condemned for eternity,
to this vile state below.
Alas, for I pity thee,
that thou shouldeth
face such sorrow e'ermore."
Behind their feet was left
the land of darkness,
For a realm of light lay ahead.
As the Holy Crucifux
And noble Caffydd gave grace to all,
They left the Realm of Dorchadais,
And returned to the Earth once more.

THEN TO A ROAD PASTORALE,
Travelled the two united,
Then along the lane through hill and vale,
As to maketh one further towards the goal,
Within all the reaches
of the Cruinne they sought
To find their way along the road.
But for Holy Light and
Holy Joy they found none,
Save a sweet Holy Rain,
which drew grace from its silence,
The aire of peace,
which Diarmuidus drew from it,
was supreme
When Ignatia fair did so proclaim:
"Look ahead dear one,
For there stands a figure in black,
Alas, that this far beyond

the Realm of Dorchadias should be found,
His servants in all their misery profound!
Give me grace oh dearest love,
For I shan't suffice to breathe
without that aid."
Yet the figure with his arms outstretched,
Proclaimed out to the couple there,
"Noble couple! I hath been sent to thy side,
By the Lord of the land beyond,
Known not as the Land of the Dead,
Yet a realm of grace and joy,
Of which thou art worthy,
For to take wicked Dorchadias head on
Is admirable indeed."
Alas for blindness,
For the hero at times canst see
what lies afore his eyes,
And this to be known by the Figure,
for it's arms stretched out again,
As from within its cloak leaped wise Cara,
Whose presence made Caffydd
sing beautifully so,
Thus leading Diarmuidus to believe.

THEN CAMETH THEY TO A LONGSHIP
    ALONGSIDE A HARBOUR QUAY,
Where wise Cara sang to the lovers,
"The Kings of Men
hath gained salvation,
Much thankful to thee,
o noble Rhygna-bearers;
So cometh to the decks of Charon's craft,
Where to reward thou shalt come,
And peace to thee shall be aft."
Then to reply sangeth Diarmuidus,
"Oh noble Cara, wise and fair,

The hounds of Hell stoodeth naught
to thy gifts,
Lead the way, wise soul,
To whatever should come."
As with before, Diarmuidus
took Ignatia's hand,
Then onto the deck of Charon,
Where awaited Cara and
the Boatmaster strong,
Their great hearts opening to the mortals,
As the sail was set, and the four made way,
Far from the Land of the Living,
Far from the Land of the Mortal.
Then into a great mist
the winds carried them,
Far across the Great Western Sea,
To a land unknown as fact to mortal men.
where no labour is needed,
Long thought to lie beneath the wave,
'Ere to bring joy to any mortal heart.
And 'twas such that Diarmuidus beheld
The land of the Holy One, the Land of God,
For as the ship came to a far distant shore
A fair green country,
on which a city was to be seen,
A city, pale in the morning fog,
like Temhair of old,
Where no army had e'er passed
nor tyrant ruled.
And there in its centre lay a harbour fair,
Wherein a quay had been built
for such ships to disembark.
And there on the shore stood Cara,
No longer the stag
as he had been accursed to be,
But now a man, of fair complexion,

the mighty,
As surrounded by the priests
and noble men of Glory was he,
Their King and Diety.
And there they welcomed the noble lovers,
As such a couple is due;
For light restoreth to the world,
As the bard sings a tale anew.

The Tale of

Eoghánë and Mæcaiteä

Death be not to love,
For 'tis an incomprehensible impossibility.
'Lo the Red Death doth not pass here,
For his sanguine splendour has no power in a world
of bliss.

It was long ago, when the world was in its infancy still, that our story doth begin. For in the seventh year of the reign of the good King Telerós of Teletír that a knight from the great moors of that same land did make his way along the great East-West Road, which led to the Seat of Telerós's realm, Dinas Fíonncydd, the greatest city the world ever hath known. Built along the River Lóthiún, it's gleaming white walls shone like the Sun for many leagues distant. Each street was lined with great trees, that bloomed at all times of the year, for they were blest by God. The many houses and structures of the city all shone like beacons of joy and happiness to the world around. At its heart stood a great hall, built from marble blocks, the size of those giants that once dwelt on the mountainsides. The hall was forever guarded by two massive statues, which flanked its front double doors, statues of great kings of old, Eilvë the Wise and Olóian the Magnificent, who had driven the evil of Dorchadias from the realm of their father Teletír, for whom the kingdom was named, five-hundred years before our tale.

The people of this land, my people, were not like the men of today, for they were filled with grace and beauty, and much less warlike than your kind. We were once known as Solasi, the Light People, when I was once in my prime nearly three thousand years ago, I was tall and fair in the face. Our people were known for our dark red and brown hair, yet some from further north had lighter snow coloured hair. Nonetheless all grew their hair, both men and women alike, longer than your own people. We loved music, poetry, and dance, and oft would be found singing as we went about our daily business. It is mournful however, for few of our songs survive today, for most are only remembered by the few who now are old enough to remember them. All the same, we spoke a language far different than that of your people. It was a tongue filled with the beauty and grace of Heaven, a tongue that had lost most words for war, most words for evil, and most words for death, for such a concept was unknown to our kind, for we had been blest with extremely long life.

Now this knight, of whom I hath spoken, was known by the name Eoghánë, which means "noble-hearted", came to the gates of the city, gates, which though forged for defence, had ne'er since the wars of old been shut. It was so that he rode through without even stopping to present himself to the guard, yet being seen wearing a knightly ring, he was allowed admittance without question. As he rode through the city, many, young and old alike, cried for joy at seeing such a man as he, for the knights of old were seen as the great heroes of the people, always being celebrated in story and song. Of Eoghánë little is known, save for he came from the province of Ardlóthiún, near where the great river meets the sea. Of his father it is not known, save that he had ventured down the river and into the sea, ne'er more to return to his native land. His mother, Nolaigiä, it is said survives to this day, yet of her whereabouts little is to be certain, for some say that upon the disappearance of her spouse, she ventured east to the darker realms and there befell the sorrow of eternal suffering. It was from her final words prior to her madness that drove the knight to come to Dinas Fíonncydd, the home of her own fathers, for here, in the heart of the realm it had been predicted:

As the peace continuith,
So too shall love flourish,
And with grace and beauty,
A prince from the river's mouth,
Shall live and love in the King's house.

Yet here too, Eoghánë was uncertain, for if he were to truly come to the city, then perhaps there would be blessings in love, for he had not yet found the one, yet with a heart that only a lover could have he continued on to the White Hall of the Kings.

Having passed through most of the city within a period of about thirty minutes, his horse, Cæpalisë, who was now covered with the petals of flowers, thrown at him by adoring crowds, with his master atop, entered the royal compound. Dismounting, Eoghánë strode towards the doors to the White Hall, yet just as he did, he beheld a beautiful sight, for there singing softly upon the green stood lovely Mæcaiteä, the King's own daughter, who sang and danced to a melody which sounded as thus:

Sharise y deróch,
A fhear eddu beán,
Sharise y deróch,
A Solasi vaith duïnë
Sharise y deróch,
Do grá ad më cantädd.

Alas for the translation of this verse is not known, yet it still shone in the heart of Eoghánë, who felt love as he ne'er had felt it before. Then through the garden he did stride towards she who had captured his heart so, yet save for her slightest of movements she did ascend, up a stair and out of sight, leaving the knight to sit in the gardens of the King, in sorrow that he had not met the fair maid.

It was late in the day when he strode down the corridor above the king's cloister, contemplating what his next service to the sovereign would be, that he heard a fond laugh. It was a soft laugh, filled with emotion and grace. Turning to find the source of such a sound he beheld the lovely Mæcaiteä, who was walking away from him down a corridor towards her study. He was in awe of her beauty, for the Sun seemed to dance off her radiant brown hair, as though it danced for her, the loveliest and fairest in all the world. Then before she could make haste from the scene, "Úndominë et Tinúfïë," he cried in the eldest tongue, "for Grace and Beauty thou art, o blessed Mæcaiteä!"

She turned, her face pure as the moon, eyes glistening like the twin stars of Pulcherrima, her lips then formed into a smile, as she replied, "And what would thee, a country knight need of me?"

"'Ere o' graceful one, I have but to stand in thyne presence and be drowned in love, be it not with ill-thought, nor with a greedy heart that I cry to thee, but from a pure heart I do proclaim my love!"

Now she was rather taken aback by his response, for few had spoken with such fairness to her afore then. Then with all the beauty of an angel, she took his hand and said, "Is misdd túdd, temomni, do captä grá meä," which translates to, "I am yours, forever, for love hath captured me." Then they went about into the cloister where beneath the shadows of the great willows, they sat and sang together.

Then lo, as the song progressed, there came one of the garda crying, "Dórbrúde is coming!" Yet e'en as the guard cried, a flock of ravens flew about the White Hall like a raging tempest, the vile darkness consuming all the joy in the Court of Teletír as once it had in the Days of Wrath. Then through out all the city the cries of fear did ring, lest some singular occurrence should unfold and in the darkest depths of fear and rage should be silenced even for one fleeting moment of certain bliss, which in its own, did but seem e'en more unlikely in these new days of darkness, which ha so thoroughly consumed the days of bliss, 'lo the changing of the tide.

Then the Lord King did cry from his lofty throne, "Who among my gallant company chivalric shall but defend my people? Who among us is brave enough for such a task?" Then after sometime he cried, "Are there but none amongst we the leaders of this land who would drive the demon from our soil? Or should the realm fall once more to the wicked ones in the darkest shadows of this Earth?

Then from the order of knights honourable did come forth, young Eoghánë Tuánstaë, lover of the King's daughter, who did call, "I, oh noble King, shall do little save the working towards Dórbrúde's own demise, for ne'er more shall these wicked ravens in flock cover the Sun ,the light of God himself, for he the brute shall fear!"

"Then let it be done, Eoghánë, Knight of Teletír, thou shalt go to the East, and not return thy person to this Hall until he is eternally consigned to shadow."

And yet, just as the champion drew his sword and presented it to the priests for their blessing, his love did enter the Hall. Hearing of what her love was to do, she began despair. But for any woman 'twould have given up all hope for love, the Lady Mæcaiteä refused to do 'gainst that. Then 'lo, as her father grasped the champion's sword, she came forth, proclaiming, "Where doth thy standard march? To which end of the Earth do you fare? Be it not to thy doom, o noble warrior of Teletír, but save thyne strength for the task at hand," then raising her right hand in salute she cried, "Hail to thee, o brave one, for I salute you!" Then the many knights and nobles of higher degree joined in her chorus, proclaiming the glory of noble Eoghánë.

Then after sometime the champion spoke, "My friends, thou merely saluteth your equal, for I am no more than that, but do know, that I shall return in peace from the East, for it shall be the downfall of evil deeds, yet now let us pray for an end to fear, an end to wrath until the world's ending!" Then all through out the hall, cries of "hurrah!" resounded, as lo the darkness seem'd but to for a moment cease. Then the King in all his glory decreed, "Then go, worthy champion, take thy steed and ride for the east, that thou may do thyne work," thien with one great hand aloft he proclaimed, "Onward, and Godspeed!" Then Eoghánë left the city and made his way to the eastern mountains, where Dórbrúde dwelt.

It was there in the dragon's lair that Eoghánë's senses first came to know fear. He great dragon of the darkness towered at 20 feet above the head of the champion. It's scaled armour covered all parts of his body, his horns the length of swords were sharper than even the greatest knightly blade.

Yet the worst was that which came from his mouth, for from the evil of his tongue shot the fires of Hell itself, destroying the lands of both the living, and some would even say, those of the dead as well. It was with speed that he disarmed the hero, driving his horns towards the defenceless. The champion lunged, and fell away from the demon, yet still he grew weary of the task.

Then the great serpent of Dorchadias rose up, preparing to strike the final blow and so lay low, the noble Eoghánë. The hero, fallen to the ground, defenceless and weakened in the arm, prepared for an eternal doom, for 'twas said that noe struck down by those who dwelt in the shadows could experience true paridise in Tíróg, for the venom in his body would also infect his spirit and make him little more than a phantom, not livin, yet not dead as well. His soul would be one of the Dór Aínm, the dark spirits who haunt the Earth, ne'er more to find peace and comfort. And yet in the Earliest Days, when the world was young, the Heavenly Father showed mercy upon the first of the Dór Aínm, granting them freedom from the Fortress of Dúin Dór and the realm of the Dark One. 'Twas said that the Dór Aínm walked the bogs, mountains, forests, and seas of the world, where even today they walk, in silence total, save once a month when the moon is greatest lit, for then they sing a mournful air, the words of which cannot be translated into any earthly tongue, living or dead, because of the greatness of its mourning.

Then with the thunders of Hell itself the great demon brought low his mighty sting upon the hero's body, crushing any hope of salvation for the knight. There in the thigh he was so infected, but scarce had he lay fallen, when his mind clouded with the curse of the Dór Aínm. He hld his breast, which seared as the heart slowed, he fell to the veil which marks the boundary between the worlds of grace and the undead. Ah, but there he heard in those searing moments of final darkness the song of a beauty immortal:

"Cantädd äddú médd,
Do grá et úndöminë ïs rígh Amat.
Et cantädd äddú médd,
Do ïs së Úndominë et Tinúfïë."

For ther stood in flowing robes of blue and white, which radiated out across the cave driving the beast further into the shadows, yet then she cried, "Depart fell beast! Leave those of the light be! For ne'er more shalt thyne presence curse the world of light!"

Then with as sigh she prayed to God in the Tongue of the Solasachi,

"Ár nÁtháir,
Saor sëi do male,
Et do ÿ áon, Tú,
mó Rí, Eddía,
Do ómnítempë."

Then the brute fell, bowing to the forces of Heaven he had so long avoided and 'tis said that there he liveth still, turned to stone, in the shape of a mighty anvil.

Yet there still lied Eoghánë Brúnhayme, his body an soul weak, yet with the power of a kiss his eyes opened and he beheld his love. "Mo Grá," he sighed, far off bordering the lands of shadow, but then she whispered into his darkening eyes, "With a kiss I give my life to you, Eoghánë, Kinght of Teletír, Guardian of the Solasachi, now live, noble-hearted one, live." Yet he sighed e'en more, drifting further from the light of Heaven, like he were drowning in the darkest depths of the sea.

It was so that with speed, the fair Mæcaiteä bore the weaken'd Eoghánë back to the White Hall, where in the shadow of death he lay, as for many days did pass, many a moon did glow, yet he ne'er roused, nor spoke a word, for the venom of the demon was great. Ah but as much as he slept, she the fair could not, for to leave his side in the House of heavlign was not on her mind, but only to save the one loved from the snares of darkness could be her goal. An aura of sorrow and grief overcame the once happy House of Rísolëve and even the good king Telerósós felt his daughter's grief.

She neither slept nor ate, drinking only a litt,e her tears cascading down her fair face, like a great river of woe. Now too, 'twas said that she lay dying, from no wound worse than the grief for a love soon lost. Her once radiating brown hair turned a pale white, her voice became soft, oft she walked about the House of Healing in silence where once there was song. It was said that with her sorrow, the joy of the entire city faded into memory, as too poor Eoghánë faded from life.

Then chance came, that a wise old priest, known as Aúddë, came to the White Hall. He was at five feet, seven inches in height and of a slender build, like not, his hair hang down to his waist. Its silver nature showed his wisdom in full. He wore an old grey tunic, which was covered by a brown cloak.

Now Auddë himself was quite intrigued on the issue of the fair Mæcaiteä, whose love for

Eoghánë was the talk of the town. Yet scarce had he questioned the most-fair, then from her lips came quivering a tale of immense beauty. Her chant enthralled and enchanted him, as the songs of old ensnared the birds, as the wind as thou know it, taught all the World to sing in distant days now passed. Yet, the Solasachi, those of the greatest minds, gained the most from that early gift. It was so that Auddë Greyglogyn, despite his many years of travel, was amazed at the beauty of the beautiful-one's verse.

When she had concluded her tale all was silent, for all that heard had a need to ponder what had been said. Then the wise-fairer said, "Thyne grief is great, thyne sacrifice e'en greater. It is due to this that he shall be spared. Worry not for him, but death on this Earth shall be the fate of you both."

She was startled by this, yet replied, "Death on Earth, I fear not, yet what lieth after doth frighten me so."

"Worry not, but follow me to the House of Healing, where e'en now, your lover awaits thee."

Then with speed they came to Brúnhayme's bedside, and with forgotten prayers said they felt the fullness of God's mercy, for in the house of the dying, Eoghánë, long thought lost, opened his eyes once more and standing with his beloved hand-in-hand, their bodies grew wings and feather'd about, they took to flight, soaring in the forms of twin swans to Heaven above.

Lovers reunited sweetly sing,
O'er the meadows of Heaven merrily,
Twin stars of Pulcherrima softly dancing,
'pon the midnight sky for e'er more.

Then through the fields and hills and glens of all the
Earth thy sing still,
A song soft and sweetly sung through the mists of
time
To Man and beast alike until to the end of days.

Other Short Stories

The Great Dance

Behind the metal edifice, which serves to both enhance and inhibit the eyes, there sits the soul of the man. Born into God's great and glorious Earth to cultivate its fields of green and tend to its rich forests and woodlands, the man for a time did his duty well. But soon the age of iron and steel drove a spike between that harmonious coupling of man and nature, granting the former more power, and the latter a life of terror and fear unbounded, ever worrisome on the matter of the very survival of the floræ.

After a time, the natural beauty of this marriage of the created began to fall apart, love replaced with economical practicality. The fullness of the nuptial pair ever shattered by the hammer and sword. The aureate age succumbing to a lesser argental time, which heralded the coming darkness. Even this new bronzed earth fell to darker times, ferric times, when the glorious golden days of old seemed a far distant past.

But even in these darkest of days, when all hope should have left man's heart, there remained a glimmer of the sun's rays. Each night, as the throng gathered together to dine following their long hard day's labours, they sang and held a ceili in the village. The dance swelled with the music, bouncing back and forth, with the jocundity of the elder days of golden joyous love.

The dance consumed the people of the village, as all joined in the celebrations. Even the wild things, the trees, and flowers, wolves, and sheep alike joined in the dance, singing in their own strange chorus, the voice of all creation, crying out to God, thanking Him for all He has given, blessing His Holy Name, and for the gift of music and song.

But then the heart of darkness came, and saw what joy filled the swilling throng, of man, tree, and beast alike. He called upon his wolves and wild things, demanding they break up this dance of life, but they too were drawn into the happy crowd. He called upon his demons, but they backed away for fear of the Truth. Then he himself approached the mass and cried out in a loud voice, "Why dance like madmen, have you lost your senses? Arbours of the woodlands, stags of the meadows, wolves and foxes of the fields and glens, why not consume man when you have the chance?"

But none could hear his cry, none even paid heed to the once illuminated spirit, none but God, who stood at the centre of the great dance, his hands outstretched, a great smile on his face, a bellowing laugh pouring from his throat, and from that laugh life was renewed to the world once more. He looked over and said to those in the shadows beyond the fire's reach, "Come, dance with me." For this once, that metal edifice was stripped away, and with his own eyes, man saw the Creator, and believed.

To Poison the Captive's Ear

In the soft meadows of Shepherd's Llyn, dwelleth a creature by name of Iúlía Albright who knew the arts of verse well that some compared her to a Meistersinger or a Dannan Elf. On one clear morn in the month of May, Iúlía lay by the llyn to play her lute which she kept atun'd to the best possible level by which the gut strings found feasible.

On llynside she sang her hymn, in her native tongue, which glowed like the Sun on a winter's day. Her heart contain'd within the warmth of her bosom swell'd with pride at the sound of each syllable. Iúlía poured out her soul from within, her immense love, her tender compassion, her sensual affection for the universe of nature, which flowed like a river of love from her being through her lips and fingers, through her harp and song, each verse with much compassionate, even at times erotic love for the Divine and Finite all the same:

"My heart, which thou hast made, O God,
is thyne to keep.
Its fruits and labours I offer in thanks.
Lets the product of mine mind and body be ever
dedicated
To thyne loving tasks that I might better serve thee
O Holy, O Omnipotent, O Loving God!"

As she sang she lay back in the grass and embrac'd the majesty of her world. All joy seem'd true, all love seem'd new, omnifelicital was her person in immortal bliss of divine ecstasy. Iúlía dreamt of expressing the depth of her love and emotion in the words, but she felt held back by her body. The muse began to feel as sense of doubt, a sense of fear of terra nullis. Iúlía's singing grew softer, becoming a faint trickle of golden song as a torrent of streaming fear filled her like a kettle one's cup. Now the llynside seem'd not as placid, for shades glided over the lake and the fairies that once danced to her golden melodies now sneer'd and cackell'd at her side. Soon the audience warp'd to a great horde and overran her bare pale feet. They climb'd ever higher on her body, consuming her legs, waist, torso, bosom, shoulders, neck and face in their rage. Then her fair skin began to resurface from beneath the torrent, at first to her relief, until she beheld their march into her being, by all means, until none remain'd at the surface.

Quiet resum'd tender peace return'd to its llynside domicile. Iúlía's breathing became evident to her as her chest rose and fell like the tide and fear played lunar dictator over the cerebral court. Then came the voice, a sound like steely frozen rain that glaciated her blood and made her breath feel feverous. "Thou art weak and feeble, little muse, nymph of the llyn. Sing not to creation but to us, thyne true masters, for thou'rt our dominion now!"

Then tears fell as her soul fought the invaders, who began to ram the portals to her mind. "I am free! Love is my standard and God my trumpeter, for He dictates the acts of my soul, dedications to His Love!"

"Love is weak!" responded the horde in unison, "Only lustful greed can bring thee liberty!"

Then into the keep they burst, as a cold flame consumed her body from feet up, driving the soul in retreat as it charged, not even stopping for breath in their venomous run. Iúlía fell back to the keep, which remained firm for now. Slowly, her cries soften'd and tears dried, until no more of herself expressed in her person. Then, the gate fell to the ram and her soul was chain'd and incarcerated in the dark places of the mind.

The Horde was brutal in governance of the body. "Now," they said in Iúlía's voice and on her tongue, "Iúlía is born once more!" She arose form her grassy bed and walked to her home, a small stone cottage cover'd by thatch. There Iúlía declar'd, "this house shall be a temple to my beauty! Lo, and list all ye who dwelleth at the llyn, no longer doth thou worship the old God, for thou hast a born goddess here on this middle-realm of reality. Adore me! O pathetic, little slaves of death!"

Then the dark fairies gathered and adored her beauty, worshipping the llyn-nymph whom they called Cybele. Then Cybele laughed in a malicious fashion as she danc'd, if one could call't dancing, about the fairies to the sound of the satyr's pope. Her body felt the addictive force of her lust and her narcissism expressed a deep desire to remain always serving her own being. Then the fairies stopped their playing, for she ceased to dance. Her voice rang out clear, "Come and relieve my limbs of their strain."

So three nymphs, enchanted as she was came forth and massaged her muscles and skin, rubbing deeply into the knots and sores, causing Cybele to cry out in pain, yet relish in an addictive joy at such harm. She screamed, yet longed for more pain, for more of this vile fire to pulse through her veins. She lay back in her cottage on the thatch as the nymphs pulsd to and from with their hands onto her thighs and feet, stabbing the most tender spots with their long and well crafted fingers.

Through the night they continued to worship their goddess, whose beauty became more and more twisted with each passing moment, that her fair white skin like ivory turned to the colour of pearls, giving off the glow of a dark damp cavern, illuminated by moonlight yet through a coloured lense of faded argent with the reflective glow of pewter. Her heartbeat slowed as time progressed, until she struggled to find the strength to continue on. Then her eyes grew wide as the Morning Star arose in the sky.

Now, through all this, Iúlía remain'd chain'd in the capital under heavy guard. She had screamed with Cybele as her body had been tormented and tortured by the Phrygian-capped invader. Now, she felt herself being pulled upwards by the Morning Star, high into the sky above Shepherd's Llyn, her arms outstretched, her legs spread, her hair billowing in a sudden wind. But as she rose higher and higher, Iúlía felt the fullness of her torment and she screamed aloud in her pain, paralysed by some angelic yet twisted power. Then at once a million knives pierced her body and blood spurted from every place. She found her screams losing power and the wailings softened, for as she look'd the star began to be overwhelm'd by a light on the horizon. Then the Sun's rays shone onto her wounds and she felt the last of the pain subside. Then Cybele looked at Iúlía in fear as the sovereign restored her throne. "Thou hath made me a goddess, but all I desire is to be queen of mine soul. Thou hath enslaved my body and my sisters, now we are free. Thou hath tortur'd me, now thou'rt forgiven. Leave in peace, dark sister! O God, let peace fall upon those who hath wrought ill!"

Then Iúlía descended to the llyn shore. She looked up at the rising Sun and blest God's Name as she sang. Then in her song she made the chorus, "Cybele, I release thee from my body in peace."

In the meadows soft of Shepherd's Llyn, dwelleth a holy beauty, a llyn-nymph and a muse, named Iúlía Albright, who devoted her days and nights to singing the lord's praises, by the banks of Shepherd's Llyn.

The Death of Colonel Mathenton

The heavy riding boots clamoured down the corridor of the jail. They were but the base of a man of great stature. He stood at nearly six feet in height, with a fair, thin, yet long face, with a most prominent nose at its centre. Such could be said of Colonel Roland Mathenton, a Knight of the Order of St Joan, and one of the favoured officers in the army of the newly established Saarlandic Republic. It had been just two years since the King had been overthrown, and with him all of the old nobility who had not joined in the Revolution. Colonel Mathenton, the second son of Baron Mathenton of Vokelby, was one such noble, who out of his own greed had joined in the revolution, taking command of a regiment in the Republican Calvary. He was renowned for his abilities as a commander of men, and gained the nickname, "The Red Colonel" for all the Royalist blood he had spilt both on the battlefield and off it as well.

For Colonel Mathenton, any and all Royalists were the enemy. In the waning years of the Revolution, as the Republicans seized control of the entirety of Saarland, in those days when the old regime's supporters held out in small pockets of guerrilla bands in the countryside, his duties changed. No longer would he and his men be "regular soldiers", for now their charge was to exterminate all traces of Royalism in Saarland, by whatever means necessary. No Royalist, or suspected Royalist was spared the price of his or her "crime against the Republic." All were tortured and killed by the Colonel and his men. At one point even, after a few months of this course of action, the new President called on Mathenton to ease up a bit on the killings, as the Republic was in need a workforce, as most of the peasantry had either been killed by the two armies, or was too weakened by age or disease to work. Thus, his course of action became one of enslavement of all Royalists who could work. The men became workers of the harvest and the factory, while the women became maids and prostitutes for the new establishment.

It was after one such raid, in which he had captured 20 Royalists, that he was seen passing down the main corridor of Saarton Jail. He had just received word that a very high-ranking Royalist had been caught in the capitol, attempting to assassinate the new President. The Colonel walked further into the depths of the lower dungeons of the prison, where could be found the various machines of torture and mutilation. His footsteps ever echoing upon the cold stonewalls. He at long last came to a door, which was guarded by a Private in a black uniform who bore the standard automatic rifle of the cavalry in his arms. He opened the door for the Colonel, saluting in the process.

Colonel Mathenton entered the dark room, which was at least twenty feet below ground. During the days of the Monarchy it had been a wine cellar for the warden of the jail. Yet now the smell of wine had long since been overpowered by the scent of dried blood that covered many of the walls. The Colonel proceeded to a man who lay on what appeared to be an operating table, onto which he was strapped down so tightly, he could only speak, yet not move his head in any direction. Colonel Mathenton always enjoyed torture, the thought of how exactly this person's life would be changed just before it's fire was extinguished forever. Almost immediately, however, the macabre smile on his face became a look of at first amazement, and later fear. "Hello, Colonel," said the man strapped to the table.

"You!" Shouted the torturer, "I thought you'd died!"

"Not yet," calmly replied the Royalist, "that is your task today."

The Colonel fell back against the wall, his eyes wide with fear. He had never experienced such emotion when first meeting his victims before, yet this was no ordinary man. There on the table lay a legend of the Counter-Revolution, a man so loved by his followers that a long manhunt had been conducted to find him. He wore the tattered remains of an old evening suit, which must have been ripped to shreds by the Republicans who had captured him. And yet, despite his desperate condition, the Royalist still held an air of grace, of peace about him. It was for this reason that the Colonel was so frightened of the man, so frightened to find the Baron Mathenton of Vokelby in his custody, so frightened at the sight of his elder brother, Maximilian.

"So, how are you, Roland?" calmly asked his brother.

The Colonel could not speak for a few moments, "I am doing better than you, Baron Mathenton."

"Come now, Roland, we are brothers, surely we can dispense of the formalities?"

"You are a traitor, and a villain, Baron Mathenton!" shouted the Colonel.

"And what, you're going to torture and murder your own brother?" the Baron replied in a calm manner.

The Colonel stalled, his mind was racing. He could remember a long forgotten day when he had played Adventures in the Colonies with his brother as children. How could he torture and kill the brother he had once loved? But then there was the loyalty to the state, his duty to stamp out all traces of the Royalists. "Where did they find you?" he asked his brother.

"In Regald's Street, near St Edmund's Church."

"Regald's Street! But they said you were trying to kill the President," replied the Colonel with a start, realising that the Presidential Palace (once the Royal Palace) was miles from Regald's Street.

"They lie, it is an affect that fear has on the mind, it helps to fabricate falsehoods. You must not trust men who have no sense of honour, Roland."

The Colonel looked in the eyes of his brother, and for the first time in years he wept. The Red Colonel wept, laying his head upon his brother's breast. The man, the monster, who had slaughtered and enslaved thousands of his fellow countrymen now felt pity for the first time in years, for a man who had long been his enemy, yet longer, though long forgotten as such, his brother. He began to untie the bands that held Maximilian to the operating table; much to the latter's surprise. "We shall swap clothes, you and I. Your face is much like my own, so now questions shall be asked. Make your way to the frontier, go abroad and live your life, Maximilian," said the Colonel in between his tears as he began to undo his coat.

Maximilian stared in amazement, "What are you doing? Why, you know I'm not going to leave Saarland, not while my task lies incomplete."

"There, my brother you are the liar, now let us get you to freedom."

The two men exchanged clothes, each looking with awe at just how similar in build and face they were. No two brothers could possibly have been as identical as them. Soon, Maximilian stood in the Colonel's riding boots, and Roland in the shredded evening suit. They faced each other once more, looking into each other's eyes. "Why?" asked the faux-Colonel.

"Philadelphos," replied the faux-Royalist, giving a deep hug to his brother, "Now go, this is your chance."

Maximilian departed from the chamber, his leather-riding boots resounding in the corridor beyond. "Leave the prisoner be," he said to the guard, then adding for the aid of his ruse "I want him to suffer alone."

Roland stood in the chamber alone; looking at its sad stonewalls. He looked down at his hands, "Many evils have been committed by these. Many crimes against God and my countrymen. Pray, o God, let me warrant forgiveness." He walked towards a device, which was the height of a man, yet shaped like a sarcophagus, which stood upright in the back of the chamber. Into it he stepped, after relieving himself of his brother's clothes. Once naked, as the device required, he closed the door of the machine, and let the serum of the torture flow freely into his veins. It paralysed first his body, making it impossible for him to scream, then forced the blood from his extremities, making them shrivel, and seemingly fade away into dust. In his last breath he felt his heart break free of his ribcage, his cursed hands become as thick as the arachnid's legs, and his eyes fall from his shrunken head. The curse was lifted, yet was Roland Mathenton truly free?

Phaëton

It hung over the streets and steeples of Kansas City like a great dark cloud, the many neighbourhoods and suburbs looking up at it in awe. It had been said by some that the airship *Phaeton* was over a mile from bow to stern, but many could not believe such a craft could ever take to flight. And yet here it was, towering over nearly half a million pairs of eager eyes, who looked up at her underside with a mix of fear and wonder. All were running out into the streets to behold the sight, businessmen and artists, cabbies peering from within their charges and clergy praying to their God at such a magnificent sight. There were scholars and vagabonds, sportsmen and aviators, soldiers, sailors, and marines on leave, politicians and pensioners, inmates and the invalid all looking upward at the great edifice in the sky. From 33rd to 54th, the city was clouded by the shadow of *Phaeton*, the greatest wonder ever built by man.

Out of his home on 55th near Main, still in his slippers ran Noël Felix, a lecturer on transportation and public efficacy at the University of Kansas City. He was in awe of the sight that rose high above his home, the great sign of man's technological achievements, which only a decade prior had been considered too fantastical to even be allocated probability within the modern imagination. "He's done it!" cried Noël, "Captain Daedalus' ship flies!" It was certainly an amazing start to a quiet Lenten Friday.

Alongside the lecturer, out in 55th Street, the many residents of the neighbourhood clamoured and shouted praises to the world renowned Captain Daedalus. It was said that he was the first person to land on both poles without stopping to refuel, the first to bring much needed humanitarian aid to the people of North Korea, the first to arrive on the summit of Mount Everest from above rather than below. Daedalus was by far the most renowned figure of his time.

~

There was a certain air about him, he did seem both kind and boastful, but not to much more than a degree expected of a man who was the conqueror of the last great terrestrial trials facing an adventurer. He had been welcomed with fabulous balls and galas in every city he visited. No less of a welcome would he receive upon arriving in the Paris of the Plains, whose artistry and musicianship were renowned throughout the world. In the great hall of the Performing Arts Centre, a great ball was held in Daedalus' honour in the evening of 31 March 2012, the Saturday following his arrival. All the great figures of the Metro were invited, the rich and famous along with those of high moral and social regard as well.

Nöel had spent the greater part of the day allocating a good evening suit for the occasion, for he was not often accustomed to wearing black tie. He arrived in the Arts Centre to hear some light chamber music being played by the house orchestra; largely at this point it was Mozart and Haydn. Upon arrival he was presented to the mayor, Edward Johnson, who had personally invited all of the guests. "Welcome, Mr Felix," he said, shaking the lecturer's hand, "I trust your father is well?"

"He is," replied Nöel with a polite smile, "he sends his regards to you and your wife."

"That's very good of him," said Mayor Johnson as he turned to converse with Walter Gregson, the famed industrialist and philanthropist. Noël gave a slight bow to the mayor and then turned and walked about the great hall. He was dazzled by the beautiful brilliance of the hall, its amazing use of glass, steel, and marble to allow for light to flood through its great open chasm that stood between the theatre that was home to the opera and ballet, and the concert hall that was home to the orchestra.

He began to walk up the stair that led to the mezzanine level of the concert hall, observing the beautiful blue shades that surrounded him. It felt as though he were walking on an aquatic azure cloud, which rang with the beauty of the music from the hall below. The swirling sounds of the strings and woodwinds mesmerised Noël, and he leaned against the wall, his breath becoming the chief function of his body, as he let the music consume his senses. The very nature of the sounds that flooded into his metaphysical soul through the all-too physical existence of the ear were enough to make even the hardest of hearts relish in the exuberance and beauty of this nearly angelic artistry.

Noël had always loved Mozart, but his life had taken him far from his youthful aspirations of soaring high above the mundane in a realm of celestial beauty, far down to labouring over improving the roads and railways of America, forming what he hoped would be a better infrastructure for posterity. And yet, despite his career baring him amongst those who are all too fond of cynical pessimism, he retained some degree of his youthful optimistic imagination, a trait which had earned great accolades for the once time pianist turned civil engineer.

Suddenly, the music picked up, a trumpet sounded in one of the higher galleries that led to the highest levels of the theatre. All eyes turned towards the grand staircase that led up to the hall from the foyer below. Noël rushed to the edge of the balcony on which he stood, peering down as a figure robed in finery processed up the stair to Mayor Johnson, whose smile beamed all the way up to where Noël watched.

His heart pounded with excitement, as he rushed down the stair to the hall, pushing his way through the mob, to the head of the stair where the adventurer stood. Though he recognised the sounds of many voices about him, he understood not any verbal expression that erupted from his fellow Kansas Citians. His eyes were on the place where stood the subject of an entire world's admiration.

The Mayor caught sight of Noël, and called to him, allowing for many members of society to steadily push the little lecturer forward, many out of a deep desire to be in his position, others simply euphoric at that historic moment in their city's history. All seemed like a daze to Noël, like a lifetime of impressionistic fog covering his eyes, the sounds of the applause and personalities about him muffled, the music slowed, yet his own heartbeat taking centre stage in this symphony of the present moment. The light about him seemed to dim as well, as he moved ever forward, to the one whom he admired most. His every thought bent on little more than his plausible reactions to the introduction that was certainly coming closer with every step.

Suddenly he was at the top of the stair, standing next to the Mayor, looking headlong into his idol's eyes. "Noël Felix, may I present Captain Amelia Daedelus."

Noël was amazed: before him stood Daedelus, not the wizened man that he had long thought, but a beautiful woman, with the steely determination of any great name from the history of humanity. He bowed low, "Captain," being the only word his tongue could emit.

"Mr Felix," she replied, with a fine mezzo-soprano voice, "it is an honour to meet you." As she walked forward into the throng, she turned to look once more at Noël, whose face by this point was a fine shade of red. She winked, then turned and walked on.

Oisín and Niamh

How Fionn mac Cumhaill the Wise came to meet
Sadhbh who would bear his son Oisín Fileidh.

In the early days of Spring when the trees
being to revive and clothe themselves after a long
and weary winter's rest, the great hall of Fionn mac
Cumhaill, champion of the High King of those days,
in the second century after the birth of Íosa Críost,
went out with the Fianna hunting. The Fianna rode
deep into the forests that covered the interior of
Éire, searching far beyond their usual hunting
grounds for a deer to claim. As they rode upon their
chariots, the warriors sang loudly, calling out to the
natural world of the gods to join them in the hunt.

It was at that time that Fionn's hounds, Bran
and Sceolan by name, who once had been men like
Fionn, caught scent of a doe deep in the wood. They
howled and barked, rushing towards the doe who
took flight at the sight of the two hounds charging
towards her. After many miles, the doe in the lead,
Bran and Sceolan close behind, and the Fianna
following after in their chariots, they came to a
river, which the doe could not cross for it was too
wide. The hounds charged forth, readying their teeth
to secure themselves within her flesh.

But it was at that moment that they found
themselves confounded, for the doe smelt not of
beastly essence, but of human. The hounds cried out
to their master, who stepped off his chariot,
approaching the weary deer. It lowered its head as
Fionn came closer, a tear falling down her face.
Fionn saw the true nature of the beautiful creature
before him in its eyes, and folding his arms about

her neck, he watched as the touch of his love transformed her into a beautiful woman.

Fionn stepped back, staring at her. "Who are you?" he asked.

"Misfortune, I am called by some. My name is Sadhbh. I come from Munster in the south."

"What evil befell you that you were forced to live in this wilderness without your humanity?"

"Fear Doirich, the sorcerer of the gods was angered at my refusal to love him. In his rage he laid a curse upon me, that until I felt love I would remain imprisoned in the form of a lowly doe."

"What poor fortune has befallen you," Fionn said, embracing Sadhbh once again. "Come, let us return to my home, where you shall live as a woman once again, filled with love and happiness."

"Let us go home," Sadhbh said, mounting the chariot with Fionn. They rode off, the Fianna behind, back to his home at Cnóc Alúine, where Sadhbh and Fionn were wed. That evening as they lay in their marriage bed, a son was conceived.

At his birth, the son was named Oisín, which means "fawn", so named as the son of his mother. Oisín grew to be a fine warrior, but more beautifully a great poet, musician, and storyteller. When Oisín sang, all that could hear would stop and listen, even the trees, birds, and beasts. The fish, it was said, would peer up out of the streams to hear his beautiful songs, much to the blessing of the fishermen.

How Oisín mac Fionn came to know Niamh Chinn Óir and travel with her to Tír na nÓg.

One day, 20 years after his birth, Oisín was running through the forests surrounding Cnóc

Alúine. As he ran, he began to sing of how Éiru created the entire world from but a little pebble in the sea. His song performed its usual magic, calling forth all the living things, florae and faunae alike, to listen. Soon he had a great entourage of wild things following along behind him, listening to his song.

At a sacred spring he stopped, offering sacrifice to the god Manannán mac Lír. As he placed his sacrifice in the spring, a voice echoed down from the other side of the water. "Oisín, you do good favours to the gods."

Oisín looked up, startled at the sound. He beheld before him the most beautiful maiden he had yet set eyes upon. For the first time, he was struck dumb.

"Have you no sweet words for me? No song to sing for such a lovely face?" she asked from atop her horse.

"Forgive me, a bhean, for your beauty leaves me without words. I know not what to say."

"Why should you sing to someone who you know not?"

"I will sing for anyone who asks of it," he replied, singing,

> All of nature sings your praises
> O beauty unknown,
> All of happiness knows your name
> Why then do I not?"

She looked down at him, a smile appearing on her ethereal face,

> "My name you ask?
> It is not from this soil
> Niamh Chinn Óir
> Is by what I am known
> Unto my father you offer

Sacrifices today
Good soul
Sing us on our way."

She jumped her horse across the spring, joining Oisín on his side. The man looked at the goddess beside him, and sang with joy. He mounted her horse, Embarr by name, behind her as they rode back towards his father's home.

A number of years later, after they had had 2 children, a son Oscar, whose name means "deer-lover" and a daughter Plor na mBan, whose name means "flower of women," late one evening in their chamber, Niamh told him of her home far across the Western Sea. She told him of how once there life lasted forever. Oisín was entranced by these beautiful tales, and said to his beloved, "Come, let us see your home, for I desire to dwell there for a while."

So a few hours before dawn they left Cnóc Alúine, and mounted Niamh's horse Embarr, upon whom they rode far to the west, until the cliffs that separate the land from the sea stood before them. Embarr charged forth, faster and faster towards the cliff. Oisín felt no fear at the side of his beloved, as they came towards what most men would cry out at, the oncoming, rushing, foaming sea. There at the cliff Embarr leaped out into the air, taking flight, soaring high above the waves, ever far away from the rising Sun in the east.

For many hours they rode across the skies, until they came to a pale of mist. Niamh cried out to Oisín, "Do not be afraid, the fogs will harm thee not." They rode through the fog, which took the breath out of both riders and horse alike. "We are almost to the shore," Niamh said, as they left the veil of fog far behind. After another hour, the trio beheld a beautiful white beach, which guarded a green forest up a hill from its sandy neighbour.

Embarr set foot on the shore, crying out with joy as he did. There at the beach a figure shrouded in mist stood, a tall spirit, who at the sight of Oisín, Niamh, and Embarr, turned, walking up the hill, running through the trees, followed by the horse and riders. They rode for hours through the forest, which despite being quite dense was luminous, as though the trees through which they rode gave off light. At long last, they reached a deep glen, which fell away from the forest with a smooth decline.

Oisín looked down into the glen, and beheld a beautiful city, which lay at its centre. The fogged spirit led them down into the glen and into the city, where they rode down the streets, until at last they came to a house near the centre. There the spirit let its veil down, revealing itself as Niamh's Father. "Welcome home to Tír na nÓg," the King said, embracing his daughter and son-in-law in turn.

Of Oisín's return home to Éire and his Death.

Three years passed in Tír na nÓg, during which time Oisín and Niamh But as the third year came, Oisín began to feel wary at being away from home for so long, especially as he had not bade farewell to his parents, family, and fellow Fenians. He decided to leave Niamh and to see his children once more at Cnóc Alúine. As he prepared to depart the city, Niamh bade him take heed of a warning, "You may return home, but know this, if you step foot on your native soil once more the weight of the years will fall upon you, and you will be unable to return."

Oisín took heed of her warning, bade her farewell, and rode off on Embarr back to Éire. When they arrived, he rode immediately back to Cnóc Alúine, his father's home. However at his arrival he was greeted by a sorry sight, for the great old fortress lay in ruins atop its hill. As Oisín rode through the great hall he wept sorry tears, realising his fate, for his 3 years in Tír na nÓg had been 300 years in his native world. Oisín rode about Éire, refusing to sing, his sorrow overwhelming his person. He knew now that his father, his mother, his children, all of his friends, had long-since died. He knew that he, Oisín, was the last one left of his time and place.

On one such day, as he wandered about the island, he came across a group of workmen who were repairing a road. He offered to help from atop Embarr, using ropes to leverage the rocks in such a way that the men could put them back into place. But the stress of the labour was too much for Embarr's girth, which snapped, causing Oisín to fall from the horse and onto the ground. At once the time that he had spent away caught up to him, as his features took on the ware and age of a 300 year old man. The sight of this terrified the workmen, who fled to the nearest village. There they called upon the local priest to come and relieve Oisín of his curse.

The priest arrived in a chariot, his robes nothing like any priest that Oisín had known. The old man looked up at his younger counterpart approaching him, though the younger man was himself reaching 70 years, saying, "What business does an exile have in ailing me of time?"

"I am here because I know you have wisdom," the priest said.

"What is your name?" Oisín asked, his voice raspy.

"I am Pádraig," the priest replied, "Servant of Dia,"

"Dia?" Oisín said, laughing mid-cough. "Which of the Déithe?"

"The one, the only, Dia," Pádraig said, looking down at Oisín. The priest smiled. "You know of whom I speak."

"Niamh's Father!"

"He is equally known to you as that. But to future generations of your race, He is known simply as Dia."

"Then what of the rest of the Déithe?"

"They are but spirits, servants of the One, True Dia."

Oisín looked up at Pádraig, as he rested on the side of the bridge. "You speak with wisdom, good priest. Now, let me rest and return to my wife and children."

It was then that time truly caught up with Oisín mac Fionn, as his weary old body faded away into dust, which his restored spirit blew in song from the shape of a circle, the sign of the Sun, forming a Cross in the middle. Thus it was that at the time of the coming of Christ to Éire, the last great poet of the ancient faith entered his eternal sleep, sweetly lying with his beloved wife Niamh, their family and friends by their side, restored to youth by Oisín's wisdom.

Abducted and Abandoned

Second Edition Publication

Light. Off to his right, light shining through the thin wispy curtains, melting into the room like a soft vanilla coloured flood on the light blue walls. His eyes opened, seeing in front of him a television, it's screen dark as the night that had since passed. The outlines of his feet visible between him and the television, under the covers of the bed, which lay like a blanket of snow atop his person, reaching up to his shoulders. Pillows propped up his head, as though laid out in ornamental fashion. At first he felt incapable of movement, incapacitated and paralysed like a city hit by a blizzard. His eyelids were still quite heavy, quite unable to fully support their weight and stay open. Worry began to spread in his mind, his imagination and reason labouring together to sort out just what had happened that he was all of a sudden in a blue-coloured hotel room. He couldn't even sort out what city he was in. Last he remembered he was in Canberra, at a meeting of some sort, probably political considering the nature of that city.

He sat up in bed, swung his legs out to the right and set his feet slowly on the floor. Standing, he went to the window, and looked out. Before him were many skyscrapers, many tall towers covered in glass, shining brightly in the radiant sunlight of the day. He walked across the room to the adjoining toilet, stopping with a startle at seeing his reflection in passing. Realising his own nakedness, he went to the dresser, opening the drawers, the returning sight being one of dismay at the total absence of any of his own clothes. Rather, the clothes he found were different, nothing like the normal sort he would wear. He quickly put them on, stopping once more at the mirror to observe the foreignness of what he was wearing, a hodgepodge of different styles and manners, with longer bright blue suit trousers, a white dress shirt that was a tad bit too small, and a shorter more petit woman's bolero. To top it all off, for footwear he could only find a pair of monk-strap shoes with very pointed toes. Thus, looking to his own observation quite ridiculous, he found a room key sitting on the table, and left.

Walking down the hall and into the lift, and down to the lobby below, he walked up to the reception desk. A woman, her nametag reading Orla, greeted him, observing the bolero, "Can I help you sir?"

"Yes, um, I was wondering if I could see a bill for my room?" he replied, wiping the sweat from his forehead.

"Certainly, sir. What's your room number?" she replied, moving her hands onto the keyboard in front of her.

He pulled out his room key, looking on the backside, frantically hoping a number was written upon it, "2505" he replied, thankful at whoever wrote the number on the key.

"2505," Orla muttered, typing it into the computer. "Ah yes, Mr Forweorthan, right?"

"Which one, there are two of us," he replied with worry, considering he didn't know to whom the room was booked.

"Alfred Forweorthan?" she replied, looking quizzical at him.

"Ah yes, that's me. I was worried that my brother Leo might have booked the room you see."

She nodded, still uncertain at his story. The bill came out on the printer on the desk. Orla took it in hand, giving it to Alfred. "Here you are, Mr

Forweorthan," she said with that ever-puzzled look on her face.

"O, thank you, um," he looked at her nametag, "thank you, Orla. You're very kind." He turned and walked back to the lift, stopping for a second with another question. "No, never mind," he muttered, continuing onto the lift and back up to Room 2505.

He sat on the bed, still unsure exactly where he was. He looked over at the television, and saw a remote next to it. Taking the remote in hand, Alfred switched on the screen and switched through the channels, looking for some sort of local show or local news programme. At last he found a local channel, where the weatherman was onscreen, "And in the next few hours, we should expect to see some clouds coming into Chicagoland from the west, which should cause rain Downtown."

"Chicago," Alfred whispered, "How the hell did I end up here?"

Alfred went about the room, searching every drawer and cabinet that he could find. Sadly, whoever had left him there had done so without leaving a penny for the poor fellow. He realised that he wouldn't be able to do anything without money, and let out a little cry, his sorrows expressing themselves for the first time.

About an hour later, a knock came on the door. It rang about the otherwise silent room, echoing in Alfred's weary head. Fear first found itself in his heart then, after all it could very well be whoever had left him in this little blue Chicago hotel room that was waiting at the door. Not being able to resist the temptation to go and see who it was, Alfred silently crossed the room, peering through the peephole. A fine feminine face with dark brunette hair stood on the other side of the door, knocking at its wooden edifice. He sighed with relief, opening it and greeting Orla with a weak smile. "Before you say anything," she said, "I need to know something – why on earth are you wearing that jacket?" she pointed at the bolero.

He reached up for it with his fingers, "I'm not sure, it was what I found in here when I woke. I'm used to wearing a suit, I couldn't just go out without a coat."

She eyed him, quizzically. "So how is it then, Mr Forweorthan, if you don't go anywhere without your suit coat, that you should only have a women's jacket here in your room?"

"Well, that's just the thing, you see I don't know how I got here either! I just woke up here not more than an hour ago, with nothing but these clothes, and the room key in here with me," he fell sitting onto the bed, staring up into her face with a pleading look. She took another step forward into the room, letting the door close behind her.

"So, you just woke up here, not knowing how you got here?"

"Yes! And here's the kicker, I'm not even sure if Alfred Forweorthan is my real name!"

"So that's why you came down to the desk! But, how could you forget your own name?"

"I'm not sure, I just don't know," Alfred replied, a curious pale of fear falling upon his face.

"Ok, so you don't know how you got here, or even your own name. Do you know what city, what country we are in?"

"Yes, we're in Chicago in the United States. I saw the weather report on the television."

"Couldn't you have figured that out from looking at the bill?"

Alfred stopped for a moment, and realising his folly he let out a momentary chuckle, "Silly of me. All that trouble and the name of this city was on a piece of paper in my hand."

"So where were you last you recall?" Orla asked, sitting to the right of Alfred on the bed.

"Canberra, Australia. I was there for some sort of meeting, probably political, I'd imagine."

"And you don't remember what you do?"

"No, not a bit of it. For all I know I could be Pope!"

"I doubt that, it sounds like English is your first language, and we all know how bad of an idea it is to have an native-English speaking pope. The last one blest the Anglo-Norman invasion of Ireland 750 years ago."

Alfred realised for the first time then that Orla was Irish. "Where are you from?" he asked, some peace returning to his heart.

"Castlebar, County Mayo," she replied, unconcerned with her own origins in comparison to the riddle that sat aside her. "Listening to you speak, I'd imagine that you are English, besides having the name Alfred. I'll guess London for now, where though in the Metropolis I can't say for sure."

"London..." he said, deep in thought, "yes, that does sound right, somewhere deep within my mind. London, it sounds nice, like sweet flowers, the sounds of a woman singing off in the garden. London."

"Alfred?" she called, snapping her fingers in front of his eyes, snapping him out of his trance-like state. "Ok, so if you're a Londoner, then the British consulate is who we'll need to go to. C'mon, I'll take you there." She took him by the arm, pulling him off the bed and towards the door.

"But, aren't you working?"

"I'm on lunch break, don't worry about me. It's you we need to sort out."

They walked out the door and down the hall, into the lift, down past the lobby, and out of the atrium onto the street below. "It's not far, just at Michigan and Ontario," Orla said, her voice raised a bit to counter the noise of the traffic on the street.

They stopped at the corner of State and Erie, just outside the hotel. Orla stood like a cat ready to pounce on a nice juicy bird, as any good city-dweller would when waiting for a light. Alfred on the other hand was shocked by all the noise. He stared up at the skyscrapers above, turning the full 360, smiling at the hotel's marquis sign, "Hotel Luna" he said.

"What?" Orla replied, staring intently at the street as the light changed, the lines of cabs roaring off like a yellow cavalry charge. She grabbed Alfred by the arm and pulled him away from the corner and across State to the northeast corner.

"The hotel," Alfred replied as they walked, "it's called Hotel Luna."

"Yeah, nice name isn't it?" Orla replied.

"Not bad, quite sweet actually."

They continued east, crossing Wabash and Rush, only turning south again at Michigan Avenue. Alfred began to look more at street level than up at the towers as they continued further from Hotel Luna, his sense that he was back in public becoming more real with each passing moment. After some more waiting for traffic lights, and working through hordes of tourist shoppers, they made it to the grey concrete and marble edifice that housed Her Majesty's Consul General to Chicago. "Inside here," Orla said, going through a door. Alfred followed her, into the building to the lifts. "You know what to say to the consul, right?" she asked, almost as a second thought.

"Yeah, I think I'll be fine."

"Grand," she replied as the lift doors opened, letting loose some office workers heading off for lunch.

They took their places in the lift and steadily rose up to the 22nd floor of the building. A suite sat opposite the lift doors across the hall, its glass doors decorated by the British coat of arms, under which read the desired words "Consulate General of the United Kingdom – Chicago". Orla and Alfred proceeded to open and walk through the double doors, approaching the receptionist's desk behind. Finding the post unfilled, Orla rang the bell on the desk, whilst Alfred paced about the room, looking at the photographs of iconic British landmarks, admiring the beauty of Stonehenge and Edinburgh Castle at the same time. They waited for a minute, until a side door opened, and a man dressed in a black business suit entered the lobby. "Good afternoon," he said with a smile in well-trained RP English, shaking both the visitors' hands. "Is there something I can help you with?"

Alfred stepped forward a bit, "Yes, um, it's a rather odd story. I am a British national, or at least I think I am. I woke up this morning in a room at Hotel Luna here in Chicago this morning, not knowing who I am, where I was, or how I got there. My friend," he turned to the woman beside him, "Orla here, has helped me sort out a few questions, but to be honest I still am in quite a bit of trouble."

"Ah, I see, yes quite strange indeed," replied the consulate worker, bringing his left hand to his chin, rubbing it as if it were bearded like some ancient eastern master. "Well, please, this does sound like something the Consul General would like to hear. We can discuss this further in there," he motioned to the door from whence he came, "If you would be so kind as to follow me."

The officeman walked back through the door and into the office beyond. Alfred and Orla followed, not quite sure what to expect. The officeman stopped about halfway across the room, turning to the figure seated behind the desk in front of the windows that looked out onto the street below. "Ma'am, a gentleman has arrived claiming to be a British national who has lost his identity, having been abducted and abandoned."

"How interesting," came a feminine voice from behind the desk. The Consul General stood, walked about her bureau and offered her hand to shake to Alfred and Orla. The Consul struck Alfred for her beauty. She stood at about 5'8", brunette hair curling atop her fair face, falling like drapery over her ears and forehead. She wore a very business-like blue skirt suit, bespoken by one of London's finest tailors. "I'm Helen Gregson, please have a seat." she motioned towards a pair of armchairs opposite her desk.

The callers sat, not saying a word as they weren't quite sure on the etiquette of the situation. "So, you were abducted and abandoned?" Gregson said, looking over her desk with firm but kind eyes. Alfred proceeded to tell her the entire story as he knew it, from beginning to that moment, making sure not to leave anything out. She seemed quite interested and curious at what he said. "And you are certain that you are a British national?" she asked, following his tale, considering that this all could perchance be a hoax.

"Well, no, you see I am not certain at all. For all I know this could be a dream, and a rather dour one at that. What proof I have you have heard in my mannerisms of speech, my accent.

"I see," she replied, turning to her computer. She typed something into it, watching as information flashed across the screen. As it did she called over to the poor man, "Alfred Forweorthan, right?"

"Yes, that's what I've found," he replied, some further concern mounting.

She looked at the screen, and then at Alfred, then back at the screen, before saying, "Well, Mr Forweorthan, it seems that you do exist." She turned the monitor about so he could see.

"That's good news, then," he replied with a smile and sigh of relief.

"It says here that your passport was last stamped in Australia, in Sydney. You arrived there on 25th May, so a week ago. And somehow you ended up here in America a week later, without any customs stamp, nor any idea how you came to be here?"

"Yes, Ma'am, that's correct."

Gregson turned to Orla, looking as if she were staring over a pair of glasses, "And what's your story, Miss…"

"Miss Dowd, Orla Dowd, Ma'am –"

She was interrupted by the consul, "Very good, Miss Dowd,"

"Thank you, Ma'am," Orla said, nodding her head slightly, "Well, I work at Hotel Luna as a receptionist. Alfred, I mean Mr Forweorthan, came down today at about 11.00 asking to see his bill. I printed a copy of it for him, and later out of curiosity went up to his room to try to make sense of this otherwise quite confusing fellow. He explained his situation to me, and I offered to help him answer his questions and find a way back home. It was my suggestion that we come here, as I guessed he was a Londoner."

"And where are you from, Miss Dowd, the Republic or Northern Ireland?"

"County Mayo, in the Republic. But I have cousins in the North, in Belfast."

"I see," Gregson replied, with an obvious air of finality, "well you can understand that I cannot be of assistance to you, Miss Dowd, as you are not a British national. However, Mr Forweorthan, I can help you. I'll put through a request for a temporary passport and a ticket to Heathrow for you, so you can at least be able to return to the UK. Do you know your home address?"

"I live in Kensington, right?"

"I'm not quite sure which neighbourhood, but I do have your address here."

Gregson handed Alfred a piece of paper, upon which she had scrawled out an address just off Kensington High Street. Alfred took the paper in hand, and looked at the ink, trying to make memories of what he read:

Alfred Forweorthan
15 Wynnstay Gardens
London, W8 6UP

"I live in Kensington?" Alfred said, looking intently at the address.

"That's what our system reads. You registered your passport to that address," replied the Consul, taking to her feet and walking about her desk towards the door. Alfred and Orla stood as well, heading towards the door that swung open at the turning of its handle by the Consul General. "I hope you find relief to your situation, Mr Forweorthan," Gregson said with a smile, "Please wait at your hotel, we will contact you."

"Thank you very much," Alfred said, nodding his head and shaking the Consul's hand with a smile, before walking out of the room followed by Orla. The Consul General's secretary, who offered them a smile as stiff as the Windsor knot that held together his necktie, saw them from the office.

Once back on the street Orla turned to Alfred, her eyes filled with a mix of concern and relief, "Well, now you know where you live," she said, tension resonating in her beautiful mezzo voice.

"Yes, you're right there. But I still don't know if that is really me!"

"That is rather a problem, isn't it," the Irishwoman concurred with a matter-of fact manner.

"I need to go somewhere where I can think," Alfred said, running his fingers through his hair, scratching his head.

"Well, what sounds like a good place to you right now?" Orla said, guiding the Englishman away from the main foot traffic.

"I do love seeing animals, fantastic animals, y'know, lions, tigers, elephants, and the like." Orla's eyes sparkled in the afternoon sun, "You have an idea, don't you?" Alfred was well aware of his companion's reactions.

"C'mon, I know where we can go."

She led him a block to the south, Alfred, though observant of her face and expressed emotions, still confused at just where she was taking him. They boarded the 146 bus, heading further south across the river and down State Street, between the great shopping palaces founded a century before by Marshall Field and Carson Pirie Scott, surrounded by locals and tourists alike, taking advantage of the department stores that lined the way. At Roosevelt Road, the bus turned east towards Lake Michigan, making its way closer to the vast blue inland sea that marks the city's end, the frontier between the manifestations of human engineering and nature's mightiest force. They left the bus behind at Soldier Field, walking across the street to their destination.

Alfred stopped and stood in front of the white classically designed building, turning to Orla, "I thought you had to work?"

"Don't worry, I've sorted that out for the day. Let's take a break from worry for a while, we both need it."

They walked up the grand marble steps, a canopy over their heads, protecting the museum's patrons from the Sun. Then through the great brass doors they strode. Alfred stood in awe of the magnificence of the great hall at the Field Museum. They bought their tickets and walked up to an information pillar, to look at the map and see what they wanted to see. Orla took Alfred by the hand, leading him towards the mammal galleries. Soon they found themselves transported from the marble great hall, whose walls reverberated the sounds of many conversations, footsteps, and children's laughter that were just as natural to that place as the smell of taxidermy to a place of quiet, whose walls were of a deep bluish-purple hue. The diorama cases displayed Asian mammals, bears, tigers, cats and furred fellows of all shapes and sizes. Alfred's face immediately released itself, allowing for the creases and lines to be relaxed and eased from their constant fury. He let a sigh of relief emit itself from his mouth, much to Orla's delight, her smile increasing with each passing moment.

They took to sitting on the benches in the centre of the hall, staring at the tigers as if expecting them to suddenly take once more to life and go about their daily lives as they did decades before, when the prowled in life. And yet, though they now stood in death in their cases, the tigers remained immortally mortal, eternally victim to that great master of all that is time. Despite the veil of mystery that separated them from the living, their scowls struck fear into the hearts of those who viewed them displayed so.

The fellows continued on their way away from the great hall, into the African mammal exhibits. Around the corner they spied the Man-eaters of Tsavo, "shot by an Irishman," Orla noted with pride, and onto the other cases on the far side of the hall. There amongst the wildebeest and zebras, the many monkeys and giraffes they strolled, with not a care in the world.

At the conclusion of the mammal halls, Alfred led Orla back towards the great hall, hoping to go and see some other galleries and exhibits. This museum was as foreign to him as just about everything else in his life at that point, and yet he still felt a sense of ease at walking the marble halls of that house of wisdom. They proceeded onto the second floor, passing by the Tibetan display, which frankly appeared somewhat confounding to their attempts to enter it. Giving up, they went onto the next gallery, which stood somewhat back from the main corridor that ran along the balcony overlooking the great hall below. Suddenly they were in a darker room, with figures off in the cases to left and right. Orla gave a brief gasp of breath, to which Alfred turned in fear of whatever it was that startled his friend. Confronting them were a set of Polynesian shields, that had quite fearsome faces painted upon them. "Not to worry," Alfred said, catching his breath, "We seem to be in the Polynesian exhibit."

"Polynesia, eh?" replied Orla, her left hand on its hip, her right hand pushing back her hair in a nervous manner, "Well, we're getting closer to Australia then."

"Australia?" Alfred gave her a quizzical look.

"Yes," she replied, her eyes flaming with certainty, "Australia, where you last recall being!"

"Ah, yes, Canberra..." he replied, in deep thought, did he really want to ever go back there, considering that something terrible must have happened to him in the Australian Capital Territory. "Come, we should be returning to the hotel, I am expecting a plane ticket after all."

He turned to go, leaving the gallery from its entrance. Orla waited behind a few moments, thinking, before following after Alfred. He walked downstairs and out the museum's entrance, not even stopping at the famed shop. The pair went down to the street, and waited for the bus to arrive.

The warm May sun bathed their faces in light as they left the shade of the canopy covering the museum's front steps. Looking at the timetable on the pole at the bus stop, Orla saw that the next bus wasn't due for another 10 minutes. "You hungry?" she asked, turning to a hot dog cart on the corner. She ordered a pair of dogs for them, bringing them back to the stop. Alfred devoured his, saying, "It's funny when one is preoccupied, I had completely forgotten food."

Orla laughed, "Well, it's good to see your senses returning."

A few minutes passed until the arrival of the bus. They boarded, and took it back towards River North, passing the Loop and its businessmen and women as they left their lofty offices in the city's great skyscrapers, heading home on the trains, buses, and braving the traffic in their cars on the expressways, tollways, and streets that radiate out from Downtown. Soon Alfred and Orla's stop came, and they disembarked, taking to foot for the last few blocks back to what was for all intents and purposes, their home, Hotel Luna.

The man at the front desk was startled to see Orla return, "Where have you been? The boss has been looking all over for you!"

"Just helping out a guest, trust me, I can explain everything to her."

"I hope so, for your job's sake. Orla, it's your first day, you shouldn't be disappearing like this so suddenly."

"I know, I know. I'll be back down in just a minute; I need to finish some things with Al- I mean Mr Forweorthan here." She walked past Alfred, leading him over to the lifts, where they disappeared from the lobby and made their way back up to his room.

Alfred opened the door, and almost stepped on a white envelope that had been slid under his door whilst he was out. He reached down and took it from the floor, a smile radiating on his face upon reading the return address label:

Consulate General of the United Kingdom - Chicago
625 N Michigan Ave #2200
Chicago, IL 60611

"It's my ticket!" he shouted, his joy radiating from all aspects of his mood, all elements of his face.

"O, that's fantastic!" Orla replied, sitting down on the bed.

Alfred joined her, opening the envelope, enclosed was a letter:

Dear Mr Forweorthan,
Enclosed in this letter you will find a ticket for the 8.00pm flight out of O'Hare to Heathrow, it will take you home to London. Your temporary passport may also be found within, it will be needed for you to make it through security at O'Hare and to board your plane. Once you have landed at Heathrow, you will not need it, as we utilise state-of-the-art fingerprint scanners for British citizens returning from abroad. Do have a safe flight home.

Kindly Yours,
Helen Gregson
Consul-General

He found the ticket enclosed in the letter, his name and everything he would need written upon it. A temporary passport was also enclosed, with a note signed and sealed by Gregson explaining Alfred's circumstances to any stingy airport security fellow. "Eight o'clock," he sighed, laying back on the bed.

The Englishman stared up at that light blue celling, thinking about the similarly coloured sky that soon he would transverse. Then Orla laid back on the bed beside him, likewise staring up at that rich light blue celling, "Would you like me to come with you?" she asked, her sweet Mayo voice quiet and soft.

Alfred rolled over onto his left, just as Orla rolled onto her right, they faced each other, laying aside each other, on that bed in that light blue room. "If you want to," he replied, in almost a whisper, his eyes softening, a warmth for his friend growing in his heart. "But what about your job?"

"It's just a job. You're my friend; I should be helping you more than working here. Plus, something about you is still quite curious to me."

"Well then, you should probably buy your ticket, before the flight is fully booked."

"Good point," she said, staring into his eyes, his deep brown eyes. Suddenly they were gone, out of her sight. Before she could sit up he was standing, "Well, if we're to leave at eight, we should get going to the airport."

"Yes," she said, still in somewhat of a fair daze, "Let's be off."

She went for the door, opened it, and was just about to let it close behind her when Alfred stopped it, "I'll see you in the lobby in say 30 minutes?"

"It's a deal," she replied, a great big smile erupting upon her fair white face.

30 minutes passed for Alfred like 30 seconds, and before he knew it he was down in the lobby, waiting for Orla. She emerged from the hotel's computer centre, a printed boarding pass in hand. Smiling as she approached him, she whispered, "I booked the seat next to you."

He smiled as they took their way out of Hotel Luna one last time, heading out onto the street. At the corner Dearborn and Grand as they waited for the crossing signal Alfred turned to her, amazed at the aura of joy that radiated from her beautiful face, crowned with such fine brunette locks, "Where to first?"

"O'Hare, of course!" she replied, turning to him, puzzled.

"But don't you have a flat, bags to pack?"

"No, I lived in the hotel. Didn't have anything of value that I'd miss," she replied as the light turned in their favour.

They continued on their way, crossing first the river and second Upper Wacker on Dearborn, before turning west, turning again a block later on Clark. They took the stairs down into the Milwaukee-Dearborn Subway, and boarded the next train bound for O'Hare. In the 40 minutes that they experienced Chicago's rush hour on the L, Alfred and Orla found themselves amused at the speed at which they travelled compared to all the drivers on the Kennedy which they passed in the middle of. The great mass of cars making their daily evening exodus from the towers of the city marked something of a daily watershed, an event that the sewer rats could set their watches to, as they planned the night's feasting upon the remains of the day's business lunches that were thrown out the backs of the city's many restaurants and bars. Soon enough they passed over the Tristate Tollway, and left the confines of the Kennedy, making its way towards the grounds of O'Hare Airport, fabled for its massive lines, delays, and unforgettable character.

They followed the signs towards the Terminals. Upon reaching the doors for Terminal 1, they looked down at their tickets, and were confused to find that they needed to be at Terminal 5. Looking around, Orla found a sign offering help, pointing all Terminal 5 passengers to take the ATS to said building at the far end of the airport. They did so, arriving at the International Terminal in a few minutes.

As they approached security, Alfred became worried at what would happen with his unsteady form of identification. He approached the security agent, offering his ticket and passport. The agent looked it over, then looked at Alfred, "I see you are a refugee, is that right, Mr Forwoerthan?"

"Yes, that's correct, sir."

The agent stamped Alfred's ticket, handing it and the passport back to him with an air of just doing his job, "Well, safe journey home then."

Alfred stepped past the first security checkpoint, hoping that no more trouble would become of him. Orla was close behind him, as they went towards the x-ray scanners, removing their shoes, belts, emptying what little was in their pockets, and making their way through the scanners without trouble. They then looked for the gate, finding it, and after spending a full 2 hours between that blue room and the M concourse gate, they at last took seats, awaiting their departure for London.

As they sat, watching the news, Alfred turned to Orla, "You say that I still puzzle you?"

"Go on…" Orla replied, turning to Alfred.

"How is it that today was your first day working at the hotel?"

Orla looked into his eyes for a minute, "I started a new job there this morning."

"And where did you work before?"

Orla sat for a moment, pondering how to answer his question, "Come to think of it," she said, her face paling, "I can't recall. I woke this morning in the hotel, the uniform in the closet, and a letter on the side table, congratulating me on being accepted as a receptionist there. I remember being from Castlebar, but not how I got here to Chicago."

They sat there together for a few minutes, in shock at realising that it was not just Alfred but Orla as well who was caught in this scheme. Soon though, before they could continue to discuss the situation, the call was made to board their plane. They did so, taking their place in the line up to the gate, walking down the jetway and onto the 747 that awaited to ferry them across the Atlantic. Alfred and Orla took their seats, 52C for Alfred and 52B for Orla, with much anticipation and excitement at what surely was to come.

At last the plane taxied out towards the runway, and roared into full glory, soaring out over Chicago, making its way northeast across eastern North America towards the Atlantic. When they were over Québec, the flight attendants came around serving dinner to the passengers. Alfred and Orla felt like they were feasting on fine delicacies from the palace, as they had only enough money between them to pay for the Underground fare once they reached Heathrow to take them to Kensington High Street. After eating, they relaxed, Orla turned on a film, her headphones in snug. Soon though her head began to lean a bit to the right, as she fell fast asleep on Alfred's shoulder, he leaned to his left, resting his head softly upon hers, closing his eyes on what had been a mad yet somewhat wretched yet exciting day. At least now he could properly say that he had a name; though for all he knew it might not actually be his. Either way there were still many unanswered questions pacing the bookish corridors of his brain as his eyes closed into a deep sleep, flying high over the North Atlantic.

Sounds. A soft soprano pierced the monotonous roar of the jet engines some twenty rows ahead of seats 52B and 52C, "Good morning, we are currently passing over the south coast of Ireland, and will be arriving at London-Heathrow in approximately an hour and a half. We will now be coming about the cabin to serve breakfast."

Alfred looked over to his left. Orla slept still, still as an infant resting in her mother's arms. He leaned in close, whispering into her ear, "Orla, breakfast is being served."

Orla stirred, her eyes slowly opening, the gentle covers gracefully retreating from her sight. Her blue eyes struggled slightly with the limited light in the cabin, their lids and lashes fluttering to allow for the pupils to adjust to their new task. "G'morning, Alfred," she said, turning to look at him. "Where are we?"

"We're over the south of Ireland, Cork I'd imagine."

"Cork, eh? Sweet people down there," she replied, yawning.

The flight attendant in charge of their section came down the row with the cart, handing a tray over to Orla, followed by a fresh banana, before asking, "Would you like some tea?"

"Certainly," Orla replied. The attendant poured the hot water into a Styrofoam cup, handing it over Alfred to Orla, then offering her a tea bag.

"I'll have a cup as well," Alfred said. The flight attendant repeated the process, handing Alfred his breakfast first followed by his tea. They breakfasted in silence, both quite hungry after six hours in the air. They continued on their way crossing the Irish Sea and skirting the south coast of Pembrokeshire before re-joining the Welsh mainland at Swansea, soaring high over South Wales until taking once more to the skies over the Bristol Channel, if only for a brief few minutes before crossing into England just north of Bristol. They soared across the South of England towards the capital, reaching London in no time at all.

The plane made its safe landing at Heathrow at around ten in the morning local time. As they reached their gate at Terminal 5, Alfred and Orla waited another 10 minutes, as they were in the very far back of the plane. After a while though, they were at last able to disembark, making their way along the left aisle way of the plane towards its front. After another five minutes, they found themselves walking on the jetway, heading towards customs. With some hesitation, Alfred made his way forward towards the fingerprint scanners, still unsure if he was really who the Consul-General had said he was. He pressed his thumb on the scanner, holding his breath. Then, joy of joys filled his heart, as a green light showed on the side of the scanner, he was through!

Looking up, Alfred saw Orla standing on the far side of the hall, having already gone through the scanners, waiting for him. "Were you that worried by it?" she asked, laughing, "If an Irish citizen like myself could make it through then surely a British citizen should be able to."

"Fair point," he replied, leading the way towards the baggage claim. They strode through the claim halls, Orla smiling at the sight of all their fellow travellers from Chicago having to wait for their bags, whilst the merry friends made their way along out of the security cleared section of the building and into the arrivals hall. They stopped for a minute outside a café, trying to sort their way about the place. Alfred looked over to his right, taking Orla's hand with his left and pointing with his right towards a large Underground roundel, "It's this way."

They walked towards the escalators, and down into the tube station. Orla asked Alfred if he could wait for her as she went to buy their tickets. He stood in the station, looking around, trying to see if there was anything about it that seemed remarkable to him from his past. The station sign seemed familiar, but then again it was like every other station's the Underground roundel with the station's name written upon its face. About 10 minutes later, Orla returned, with a pair of travelcards, "These will be more useful than just single tickets," she explained. They went through the turnstiles and waited on Platform 5 for the next train into London. Alfred looked around, somewhat bored by the empty concrete wall opposite the platform.

He turned about, catching his reflection somewhat in the ever-so-reflective off-white almost greyish tiles on the platform side of the tunnel. The Englishman was surprised to see that he needed a shave, and a shower. His face was worn by the travelling and worry that came with not knowing 24 hours before just who he was. Orla watched him, realising that he was not alone in his confusion, in his wonder. How could she have forgotten, how could she have not even noticed that she too couldn't honestly recall what she had been doing more than a couple days before either. Had she too been duped by the same scheme as Alfred? As a tear appeared in her eye, the train arrived at the platform. They boarded it, taking seats near the front of the third car so that they could get some breeze.

Some 40 minutes passed, as they made their way through West London. People got on and off of the train, the crowd ever fluctuating and changing as the stations came and went. At Earl's Court they switched trains, from the Piccadilly to District line. The announcement for "The next station is High Street Kensington" took Alfred by surprise, as they had been travelling now for what seemed to be about 10 hours without so much as a stop. They exited the train, walking up the steps from Platform 2, making their way up into the Kensington Arcade. Once out of the crowd of midday shoppers and on the street, Alfred realised that he hadn't a clue as to where they had to go. Standing at the entrance to the station, they looked around, searching for some sign of exactly how to get to Wynnstay Gardens, which had to have been close, after all High Street Kensington was where they were recommended to take the tube to, but in all the high street hubbub, the pair found themselves lost.

After ten minutes of standing, leaning against the arcade's walls, a policeman came over, "I'm sorry, but I'm going to have to ask the pair of you to move along," he said, briskly.

"Sorry, sir," Alfred said, "But we're just off the plane from Chicago. We're supposed to be meeting some friends in a house near here, you wouldn't happen to know how to get to Wynnstay Gardens would you?"

"Wynnstay Gardens, eh?" the constable said, "It's just a few streets that way," he pointed towards the west." Go down the high street to Allen Street, then turn left there and take the next right onto Wynnstay Gardens. Good luck," he said, walking away into the station, describing Alfred and Orla to the people on his radio that rested on his shoulder.

They followed his instructions to a tee, walking along the High Street until they reached Allen Street, at which they left the mass of businesses and shoppers, proceeding into the quieter daytime neighbourhood. At last they turned onto Wynnstay Gardens, finding a fine Victorian red brick building facing them, the number 15 proudly hanging on its front, in all its finery and glory. Alfred approached, quite unsure at what to expect.

As he reached the front door, he turned to Orla, a look of terror on his face, "I just realised, I haven't a key!"

Her face joined with his in its terror, "Don't worry," she said, reassuring both of them, "Just knock, let's see if anyone's home."

Alfred turned once more to the door, his hand hovering in front of it. He formed a fist, and let it fall thrice upon the wooden edifice, its thick old oaken manner resounding his drum-like beat. A pair of footsteps approached, and the form of a figure became visible, a halo seemingly appearing about it with the front hall light glowing behind. The door opened with a creak, as an elderly woman appeared standing before the couple, "Alfred, Orla?" she asked, "Why, you've been away for quite sometime!"

Alfred stared into her aged face, at her eyes, trying to decipher the clouded mists that prevented him from recalling her name. Orla returned him from his thoughts, "Yes, we've been in Australia and America. Sadly, somewhere along the way we lost our keys. I trust we still have our flat?"

The landlady looked puzzled, "Why of course you do! It's only been a month after all!"

"Yes," Alfred said, "it has been a month, hasn't it. Well, that is something," he walked passed the landlady and into the hall. Orla followed him.

"Well, if you'll excuse me," the older woman said, "I'll just go and fetch a key for you." She went down the hall and through an open door at its end.

"How did she know me?" Orla asked, confused.

"I was wondering the same thing," Alfred said, as the landlady audibly fuddled about in a desk, looking through her keys. "Perhaps we were friends before whatever happened to us."

"Must have been," Orla said, turning away as she went over to look up the stairway.

The landlady returned, "Now not to worry, nothing of yours has been moved or meddled with, I've left it all how it was when the pair of you left." She led them up the stairs, stopping at a door at the top of the flight, entering the key into the lock, and turning. A click sounded, and the door swung open with a turn of the handle. "Here you are," she said, moving to the side of the door as Alfred and Orla entered, "I do hope you had a good time abroad."

"Thank you, we certainly did!" Orla said, smiling.

"Well, I'll leave you to it then," the landlady said with a sigh, heading back down the stairs to her flat below.

Orla closed the door behind her, turning on the celling light. Alfred was across the room by the window overlooking the street below, a framed photo in his hands, "Orla," he said, his voice cracking.

"What is it?" she asked, coming over to him. She looked at the photo in his hands, a gasp forcing its way from her breath as the caught sight of the people in the photo. There stood Alfred, in a morning suit, a beautiful white rose in his lapel. Next to him was Orla, in a fine white dress, her veil back off of her face over her hair, a bouquet in her hands.

"We're married!" they shouted, starring at each other, the confusion mutual, the shock and fear at such a realisation hitting them like a tonne of bricks. They sat on the sofa, staring out at the flat before them. It was a nice place, with mid-century wallpaper lining the space, the odd photo and painting here and there, presumably of each other's families.

That wallpaper, its floral pattern resonating like their heartbeats, echoing throughout their eardrums, like the tapping of some forlorn Richard-like prisoner on the walls of his cell, deep in a cavernous antechamber to the grave. It seemed to go on forever, the pattern on the walls, forever and ever, like space and time itself, like all the things born, living, dead, and yet to be born. It was like all reality plastered there onto some sheetrock, nailed onto the wooden beams below, demarcating the division between drawing room and kitchen, kitchen and bedroom, bedroom and toilet. It filled Alfred and Orla's eyes, flooding them with green and yellow leaves on a field of grey. Tears came to Orla, tears that ran down her cheeks, like a torrent, a Reichenbach of emotion covering her cheeks with water. "I remember," she said, her voice quivering with the lump that had invaded and annexed her throat. "I never liked that wallpaper."

Alfred turned, looking at his wife's ever so beautiful face, "We were going to get rid of it weren't we?"

"We were," she replied, wiping the tears from her eyes. She stood, and walked into the bedroom, turning the door's handle with a creak, after all it hadn't been used in a month. She went and laid down on the bed, still dressed. Alfred stood, following her into the bedroom. He stopped at the foot of the bed, looking intently down at her face. She was still awake.

"I'll put the kettle on," he said, turning to leave.

"Alfred -" she called.

"Don't worry," he said, turning, "Rest for a while, I'll keep yours hot."

He lit a match, lighting the cooker, filling the kettle with water and letting it heat up. He sat down at the kitchen table, as there was no dining room in their flat, and tried to sort out in his mind what all had happened thus far.

26 hours ago he had woken at the Hotel Luna, in Room 2505, a room with a very light blue colour. He met Orla at the front desk of the hotel when she printed out his bill, which provided him with his name, Alfred Forwoerthan. She then proceeded to follow him up to his room, where she decided to help him. They went to the British Consulate, met with the Consul General, an Ms

Helen Gregson, who provided Alfred with a plane ticket to London for that evening. After the visit to the Consulate, they took the bus down to the Field Museum to relax a little. They had then returned to Hotel Luna, where Orla booked her own ticket on the same plane, somehow, considering it was at the last minute, in the seat next to Alfred's, and they took the L up to O'Hare where they caught their plane to Heathrow. They dined over Québec and breakfasted over Cork and Pembrokeshire. 3 and a half hours ago they landed at Heathrow, made it through customs thanks to the European Union fingerprint scanners, and took the tube to High Street Kensington, where they got directions to Alfred's flat at 15 Wynnstay Gardens. They made it into the flat without any trouble, and discovered that it was not just Alfred's flat but Orla's as well, because they are married. "And now my wife is sleeping in the next room while I'm out here with the kettle," Alfred thought to himself.

Just as that thought simmered in his mind, a shriek came from the cooker. He had forgotten about the kettle, focusing more on the wife part, a fact that still had to sink in. Alfred briskly went over to the cooker and took the kettle off of the flame, putting it out quickly. As he poured the water into two teacups, a voice came from the other side of the kitchen, "Are you making some for me too?"

Alfred turned, Orla was up, awake, though still slightly groggy. "Yes, of course," he said, bringing the two cups to the table. He sat them down, taking up the box of tea bags, choosing a white tea for himself. He handed the box to Orla, who likewise picked a white.

"I know where we need to go, to figure out what happened to us," she said, blowing onto her tea that it wouldn't scorch her tongue.

"Where?" he asked, setting his cup on the table, looking intently at Orla.

"It was near Old Street, I'm sure of it."

"Old Street?" he was confused at first, "O, yes! I remember that scientist, doctor of sorts had his office near the Old Street station."

"Quite," Orla said, sipping her now sippable tea. "We should be going soon. I think I remember where it was, it wasn't too terribly far from the station there."

"You know something, Orla, we could very well have just lost a good deal of our life to whatever caused us to lose our memories. How easy do you think it is for a married couple, a couple who, as it seems, was quite in love, to forget about each other? How is it that we spent all that time together yesterday yet didn't even realise who we were until we got here this afternoon? It just doesn't make sense. It doesn't even feel like I'm looking at my wife. Frankly, I'm just bloody well confused right now," he said, standing, his irritation peeking its unwelcome head out from its slumber.

"Let's go and see this doctor, maybe he'll be able to help us," she replied, looking up at him, "Alfred, it's our best chance yet."

"Do you remember his name?"

"Colin Fleming," she said, standing and walking towards the front door. "We should go now, before rush hour starts."

Alfred followed as they left their flat, Orla keeping the keys in her inside coat pocket. They walked out onto the street, making their way back to the tube station on the High Street.

Once they were back in the tube station, Orla led the way down towards the Circle line eastbound tunnel at Platform 2. They sat and waited for a few minutes for the train to arrive, their hands tightly grasping that of their spouse, as their eyes darted about the platform. As time passed it began to fill with more and more people until the concrete platform was full of businesspeople and other workers leaving Central London for the night. After five minutes of waiting the train finally appeared from the depths, the clinking of its wheels upon the rails, the machinations of some engineer some years before roaring into sight, the breeze it generated relieving the hundred or so people on the platform of the strenuous heat that had overwhelmed the otherwise breezeless tunnels of the tube in the summer rush, the mass of hot bodies, healthy and ill alike generating the heat so desired only a few months prior in the depths of winter.

The train came to a halt, letting the doors open and a stream of commuters and tourists alike flood out of the carriages and onto the already crowded platform. Orla and Alfred moved closer to a train door, sliding between a pair of men in suits as they stepped up onto the train. Orla walked down to the end of the carriage, waving to Alfred to follow her. She stood in front of the door at the end of the car, sliding open the closed window. As the train doors closed she let the doors to her sight slide shut as well, keeping her eyes from watering at the sudden burst of cool air that came from the now open window behind her. Alfred stood in front of her as they sped towards Gloucester Road. At South Kensington the crowd of tourists lessened a bit, with families and students alike taking their leave of the Underground to see the museums above. They rattled on their way east, through Sloane Square and into the City of Westminster. At Victoria Station the train crowd dispersed, the masses flocking to the national and suburban trains above. They were replaced by yet an even larger crowd, which piled onto the train, filling it comfortably as it made its way under the halls of power in Westminster and along the Thames through Embankment, Temple, Blackfriars, Mansion House, Cannon Street, finally arriving at Monument. Alfred and Orla made for the door, stepping off the train to find a platform filled somewhat with men in black suits. As they stepped off the train, Orla looked up to her right at a sign over an archway just next to them reading "To Bank". She grabbed Alfred by the hand, leading him up the stairs, around the bend, and up the next flight of stairs into a foot tunnel, which led them into the busiest station thus far.

The city bankers appeared all about the couple as they arrived in Bank station, it's halls filled with men and women in suits. Alfred and Orla made their way towards the Northern Line northbound platform, where they just barely caught the next train out of Bank. They found themselves once again forced to stand, as the minimal seating was already quite well taken. Yet this time there was none of that relieving breeze, as they were stuck near the main doors in the centre of the car.

Alfred leaned up against the wall as Orla held onto one of the overhead bars. They sailed along, stopping at Moorgate before making the final trek under City Road up to Old Street. After stepping off of the train they made their way up a flight of stairs and into a pedestrian tunnel, curving around its platform-bound sister, until they reached the escalators at the tunnel's mouth. Once up the ever rotating escalators, they walked through the turnstiles and out into the shopping centre beyond. They stopped just outside the station, in front of the gathering evening newsstands and station coffee shops, looking for the way out. Orla walked over to the coffee counter just to the right of the station's entrance from that vantage. She stood at the counter for a minute, queuing behind a woman who had just ordered an espresso. After the woman had paid and left, the woman behind the counter turned to Orla, "What would you like?"

"Hi," Orla began, looking up at the menu above the clerk's head, "Could I just get a bagel?"

"What kind?" the clerk dryly replied.

"Um, walnut would be nice."

The clerk looked at Orla with some amusement, "Walnut it is then." She pulled one from its home under the counter, dropping it into a bag. That'll be £2.50."

"Right," Orla said, taking a £2 coin and a 50p from her handbag. She set them onto the counter, from whence the clerk retrieved the coinage, dropping it into the till. She turned Orla, confused by her continued presence in the café.

"Something else?"

"Um, yes. Could you tell me how to get to Hoxton Square from here?"

The clerk smiled a bit, "Just go down this tunnel to the right of my counter, and take the right when you reach the end. Then follow Old Street until the new hotel at Pitfield Street. Take the next right off Pitfield Street onto Boot Street, go through the Market with the juggler statue, and take the right at the far corner of the market. Got it?"

"Yes, thanks!" Orla said with a smile, turning and walking away from the counter and down the tunnel, Alfred by her side.

"And welcome to London!" the clerk called after her with a laugh.

Alfred and Orla followed the clerk's directions to a tee, coming up the pedestrian ramp out from the roundabout shops and tube station and into the greying cloudy London afternoon. They walked along Old Street, passing by a pub and a line of kebab and fast-food places as they went. They could smell the aroma of the meats and chips cooking for that evening's clubbers. As they continued on their way they came to a more open area, with trees separating the main pavement along the street from a sort of walled court, its walls painted with scenes from the history of the neighbourhood. They pressed on, passing a set of cafés, restaurants and pubs, before passing a grocery and coming to Pitfield Street. They turned the corner, dodging a pack of cyclists before making another turn onto a smaller, cobbled street that ran behind the new hotel and in front of Hoxton Market. Alfred made to turn into the first open courtyard, but Orla stopped him, pointing out that there wasn't a statue in sight. After a fashion they turned into the proper market, walking past the juggler statue, admiring its grace and form. There were tables and chairs outside a café that sat in the statue's shadow, with locals sitting about the tables drinking tea and coffee in the afternoon's glory. Among them were a table of three American women, discussing their classes at one of the local universities and where they were going to go that evening. It sounded to Alfred and Orla that a play was in order for the students, who were obviously enamoured with London and its pace of life.

The couple continued onwards, passing through the market and out into another alley-like street towards far greener pastures. Soon the alleyways receded and revealed to them a beautiful green square, its trees shading the locals who leaned against their trunks, some reading, some painting or sketching the scene, others talking to each other with grand smiles on their faces. All was happy here, simply sublime. The aura of their joy oozed over Alfred and Orla's complexions as they too began to smile broadly, grasping even tighter each other's hands as they strolled down the street and across the green. Their relief was further settled as they at last came to the house they had been looking for. In front of them stood a shorter, older, yet beautiful house, it's number reading "39". They walked up its gate, unlatching it, letting it swing open, and going to the door it guarded. Orla rang the bell this time, hearing a faint buzz from inside.

Footsteps approached the couple, leading to the door unlocking and swinging open. A man in a greyish-blue suit wearing a white shirt and soft green paisley tie answered the door. He had greying curly hair that mounted his long lean pale face. His hands did not seem worn at all by his work, rather they were soft, without too many wrinkles. He looked out at the couple, his eyes widening, "Can I help you?" he asked in a baritone voice.

"Hello, yes, well it's rather hard to explain," Orla stammered.

"I'm sure it is," he said dryly.

"You see my husband and I recall visiting a doctor here sometime ago, and we wondered if we could speak with him again. Is there a doctor who works at this address?"

"Yes."

"Would he be able to meet with us?"

"Perhaps."

"Could you take us to him?"

"I can take you to his office. He will speak with you there."

"That would be lovely," Orla said, following the man into the house with Alfred right behind her. They walked down the front hall and into what seemed to be a drawing room behind. The man held his hand out, motioning for them to take seats around a coffee table. He then took a seat opposite him.

"Now, what may I help you with, Ms Dowd?"

"You're Colin Fleming!" Orla cried, a scent of shock in her voice,

"Yes, I am Doctor Fleming, the one who operated on you both," he replied in a matter of fact fashion.

"Operated," Alfred said, fear in his voice, "On what?"

"On your souls," the doctor replied.

Alfred and Orla stopped for a moment, fear filling their hearts, expelling the joy that had previously taken up residence in their persons. "I don't understand," Orla said, almost too fearful to learn anymore.

"I am a doctor of souls," Fleming replied, his hands perched in front of his chest in a triangular Holmesian fashion. "I cure people of the ills that penetrate their deepest beings, that form their deepest desires. Some say I kill, that I am a murderer, a usurper of power that should be reserved for the divine alone. But I say that I save, I save lives and joys –"

"What did you do to us?" Alfred shouted, unnerved, "A day ago I didn't know who I was or where I was! A day ago I was nobody, so if you don't mind, I'd like to know what happened that I lost my identity!"

Fleming replied as calm as ever, "I saved you both. I saved your marriage, your love. Consider the fact that despite the pair of you not knowing that you were married until just a few hours ago it was each other that you met in that hotel in Chicago. Consider, if you will, how strange it is that out of the billions of souls on this planet, that your two souls are drawn specifically to each other. You volunteered for the operation, and you both succeeded. You have proven that there is something physical, something scientific about love and passions.

"When you came to me a month ago, your marriage, which had stood strong for five years was on the verge of collapse. Alfred, your work had taken you to all corners of the globe, meeting with key allies of this country and working out just how to keep those alliances and partnerships in cheque. Orla, you were here in London, ever hard at work in the Foreign Office. You saved many British citizens abroad the trouble of being stuck in counties deep in revolution and civil war. Both of you were strained, worn down and weary. I saved your marriage the only way I could."

"How?" Orla asked, tears streaming once more down her face just as they were down Alfred's.

"I gave you both a fresh start. I induced sleep onto both of you, as I would in a surgery, and using a sort of laser that I invented, I removed your souls from your bodies, and placed Orla's soul, Orla's self into Alfred's body and then placed Alfred's soul into Orla's. Alfred, you are she. Orla, you are he."

Light. Above her, softly glowing a light bulb sat perched over Orla's head as her eyes fluttered back into sight. She let her head, which had fallen back to rest on the top of her chair, return to its normal placing. Before her sat Dr Fleming, still with his hands perched beneath his chin. She looked to her right, looking for her love, for her darling Alfred. He had fallen onto the floor of the room, his panic inducing him to sleep. She stood, suddenly feeling a sense of dizziness. She walked over to Alfred's body on the floor, kneeling down to touch his shoulder.

"Don't," Fleming commanded.

Orla looked up at him, "Why? Why would you force us to switch bodies? What good would that do?"

"My dear lady, or should I say sir, I saved your marriage, I saved your souls from the horror of separation from their mates. I kept you both from terrible pain —"

"But our souls! Doctor, these are not just organs that can be donated from one person to another, these are our souls!"

"It was what was best for you both," he said, rising. He walked over to Alfred's body, leaning over he took the man's arms, raising his eyes to Orla, "take his legs, we'll set him back up in his chair."

They did so, setting Alfred comfortably back in his seat. A few moments later he awoke, dazed at the fall. He turned and saw Orla standing next to him, "My dear," he said, standing and embracing her in a big hug, "I just had the most terrible nightmare. That Doctor, he said that he had switched our souls, that you were me and I was you –" he stopped, seeing Fleming sitting before them. Alfred raised his arm, pointing his finger at the seated man, "You! You did this to us!"

"Do take your seat, Orla," the Doctor said, looking at Alfred. The standing man stopped, staring at the Doctor, he began to sob, to cry relentlessly, his tears falling swiftly down his cheeks. The woman went over to the man, taking his weight and helping him to sit. After a minute the man quelled the flood. He looked Fleming in the eye, "I want you to give us our bodies back," he said, with force yet still a quivering lip.

The woman gave a similar look at Fleming, "Yes, if you can switch our souls one way surely you can do it in reverse."

"If you two insist, then it will be done. But be warned, the after effects that you felt last time could happen again."

"Then at least do us the courtesy of making sure we wake up in our own flat and not a quarter of the way around the world."

"I will do my best. You see last time you appear to have woken a week earlier than expected. You both may not remember it, as the process takes longer than just the operation in this house, but mid operation both of you decided to flee the country. You first went to Australia, and then to America, where in Chicago you both woke in separate rooms in Hotel Luna. This time I will make certain that you both sleep the entire time of the transition, so that no such occurrences happen again."

"Very well," the woman said, "So what should we do?"

Fleming stood, showing them down into the cellar. There he had them undress and put on hospital gowns. He then took the woman first into a room where an operating table stood with a sort of dentist's light hung overhead. Once inside he powered up the machine, put the woman on a breathing machine, and performed the operation on her. Then he took her from the table, into another room where he laid her in a bed.

He then returned to the operating theatre's antechamber. The man sat, nervous, quite nervous. "If you would please follow me, Ma'am," Fleming said to the man, taking his arm and helping him into the operating theatre.

The man laid back on the table, breathing heavily as Fleming began to lower the breathing mask over his head, "Will this hurt?" the man asked in a small, fearful voice.

"Not a bit," Fleming said, smiling, "Now go to sleep, Orla Dowd. All will be well when you wake."

Light, slowly dimming, as if covered by a thin layer of fog. Light, fading now, fading into darkness. The land of the living giving way to the land of dreams.

Nothing thereafter was heard of Alfred and Orla Forweorthan, no articles in the papers, no international whispers. Only the stories of their neighbours, of the children who grew up on their street, about the lovely couple, who lived happily together for 70 years. They spoke of a husband, of a man who was said to understand his wife fully, and of a wife who felt the same of her spouse. One neighbour was said to have surmised them as such, "No other couple could have so fully been happy as they were, or so equal as they saw each other. Neither husband nor wife had domain over the other; they both lived out their lives happily in perpetual light.

About the Author

Seán Thomas Kane is a poet, playwright, short story author and reviewer. He has written 14 plays to date, hundreds of poems and a good number of short stories. He is best known as a historian, political analyst, and as a polyglot. Kane earned his B.A. in History and Theology at Rockhurst University in Kansas City, Missouri and his M.A. in International Relations and Democratic Politics at the University of Westminster in London. Kane lives in Kansas City, Missouri.